THE PARAMEDIC'S PARTNER

CONTEMPORARY CHRISTIAN ROMANCE

FULLER FAMILY IN BRUSH CREEK ROMANCE

BOOK FIVE

LIZ ISAACSON

ISBN-13: 978-1638760917

"Lead me in thy truth, and teach me: for thou art the God of my salvation; on thee do I wait all the day."

Psalms 25:5

Chapter 1

Fabiana Fuller groaned, the light coming through the window like daggers to her aching head. It was more of a stabbing pain pounding through her temples, and her stomach cramped uncomfortably too.

"Jazzy," she moaned, hoping her twin was still in the room somewhere. She vaguely remembered hearing the squeak of the door as it opened, but that could've been yesterday. Or last year. Maybe another lifetime.

Everything hurt, but Fabi managed to push her legs over the side of the bed and use her hands to get herself into a sitting position. Her vision swam, and she lay back down.

This couldn't be happening, but a late spring flu had been making its way around Brush Creek, taking down the Chief of Police, her mom, the pastor, and now, apparently Fabi herself.

"Jazzy," she tried again, this time rewarded with that squeak that annoyed her sister but that Fabi actually found comforting. After all, no one could come in their shared bedroom silently, and Fabi's overactive imagination sometimes had someone trying to abduct her in the middle of the night.

"You're burning up," Jazzy said, her usually playful voice nowhere near jovial now. "I'll call Wren."

"Wait." Fabi curled her fingers around her sister's wrist. "I have a date tonight."

A beat of silence passed before Jazzy said, "So? You can reschedule."

Fabi shook her head, but that made the whole room spin violently, and she clamped her eyes shut. "I can't. I've already done that twice. He'll think I'm not interested."

"Surely whoever the flavor of the week is will understand the flu." Jazzy spoke with enough bite to add to Fabi's headache. Fabi didn't blame her, but it certainly wasn't her fault men asked her out instead of Jazzy.

"It's that cute paramedic from the park," she whispered to her pillow. "I really wanted to go out with him." And her stupid work schedule over the past two weeks since the pet adoption in the park had kept her from making her previous attempts to meet Max.

She'd been cleaning up flu germs for everyone from the river to the horse ranch up the canyon. No wonder she felt seconds away from passing out.

Somewhere in the haze of her flu-ridden mind, an

idea formed. "You have to go," she said, tightening her grip on Jazzy's forearm.

"No." Jazzy tried to shake her hand away. "He doesn't want to go out with me. Remember how he met us both and only had eyes for you?" So there was some bitterness in Jazzy's voice. Fabi heard it, didn't know what to do about it. Jazzy was the flirt, and she usually got the men to come over and meet the sisters. But it was almost always Fabi who walked away with a date.

Honestly, the whole charade was getting old. Fabi couldn't even count how many first dates she'd been on in the past year. Probably fifty. Maybe more. It was getting to the second date that was hard.

She *could* count those. Two. Two second dates in the past year. Zero third dates. She wasn't sure what was so wrong with her, but somehow, she believed she was fundamentally flawed.

But Max had been different.

"Please," she begged, only able to say one word through the fire in her throat.

"I don't even look like you." Jazzy stopped trying to get away, and Fabi relaxed a little too.

"Go see Starlee. She can replicate my A-line."

"I don't want to dye my hair."

"It's a few streaks," Fabi said, opening her eyes. "Please, Jazzy. If I don't show up or if I cancel again, I'm sure it'll be over."

"Maybe it should be. I mean, if the guy can't understand the flu." Jazzy sat on the edge of the bed and stroked Fabi's hair off her feverish forehead.

"Just one dinner," Fabi pressed, sensing that she almost had Jazzy convinced. Growing up, the twins had loved switching places, going to each other's classes, trying to fool their friends into believing they were someone they weren't.

They hadn't really taken the practice into adulthood, but then again, the situation had never demanded it.

But this one did.

Fabi pictured Max, who was big, broad, and bald. She'd been immediately attracted to him as he worked with the dogs that were up for adoption. She and Jazzy had a cat, and Marbles would definitely not appreciate a canine companion, but Fabi had played her cards just right, showing just enough interest in the dog to capture the attention of the man.

"He's taking me to Clive's," Fabi said, hoping that would seal the deal. Of course, her sister would have to do their normal housework alone—which she hated— and get her hair cut and colored before six-thirty. But it was do-able.

"What about the mole?"

"He won't notice."

"What if he does?"

In moments like this, Fabi wished she could get the fingertip-sized mole behind her right ear removed. "He won't," she said. "Because you'll be witty, and charming, and flirty—you know, you'll be yourself—and he won't notice."

Jazzy fell silent for what felt like a long time. "But that's not how you act," she finally said.

"You're right," Fabi said. "You better pull the flirting back a bit. And the giggling." Her twin giggled entirely too much. "And no kissing him."

"Why not?" Jazzy said, standing. The movement jostled Fabi, who groaned as discomfort swept through her. "You kiss on the first date."

"Not this year," Fabi said.

"Please." Jazzy scoffed and her footsteps moved away from Fabi's bed. "You kissed Mason Limebert last weekend."

"And he didn't call me back," Fabi said, another pinch moving through her that had nothing to do with the flu. So she wasn't perfect. Maybe she came on too strong. Maybe she had a reputation of kissing on the first date and that was all the men in this town wanted.

"Jazzy?" she asked when she didn't hear the squeak of the door.

"I don't think I can," she said.

"Of course you can." Fabi lifted her head and squinted, wondering how sunlight could hurt so badly. "It's totally do-able, Jazzy. Please." She couldn't quite see Jazzy, but she heard the squeak as the door opened.

"I have to go call Wren." The door clicked closed and Fabi let her head fall back to the pillow before pulling the blanket over her eyes to drown out that merciless sun.

Wren managed all the jobs for A Jack of All Trades, the family company that Fabi and Jazzy worked for. They cleaned all the residential accounts in town, in Beaverton, and even up in Maple Mountain. It was Thursday, which meant their schedule was jam-packed, and Jazzy would never be able to get all their work done, get her hair colored, and be ready to meet a man by six-thirty.

Please, she prayed, her fall-back whenever she couldn't quite make a situation do-able in her mind. But God could make anything do-able. *Please have everyone cancel for today.*

If God was a God of miracles, and Fabi believed He was, then when Jazzy called Wren, she'd find out she had plenty of time to get her work finished and get her hair cut into the stylish A-line bob Fabi had adopted three weeks ago, streaks and all.

———

FABI HAD a unique talent to think anything was do-able. Jazmin Fuller, on the other hand, did not. The thought of squeezing in a two-hour appointment at the salon had her teeth clenching while she waited for Wren to pick up.

Her sister answered with a harried "Hey, Jazzy," while a toddler screamed in the background. "What's up?"

"Fabi's not getting out of bed today," she said. "She's got the flu." Jazzy wandered back over to the bedroom doorway and peered inside. Fabi lay perfectly still, her eyes closed and her face gray. A prick of concern touched her heart. "I'm not sure she should be left alone, honestly."

Wren exhaled and grunted. Etta quieted, though her soft sniffling could still be heard through the line. "Well, we got lucky," Wren said, her voice slightly muffled. "Dottie and the Fierios canceled for today."

"They did?" Jazzy couldn't believe Dottie Tanner had canceled. Jazzy and Fabi had been cleaning the older woman's house for a decade, ever since she was their youth leader and her husband had passed away. The Fierios were hit and miss, and in the summer, they were sometimes gone for weeks at a time and did cancel their maid service.

"Dottie has gone to her daughter's for the weekend," Wren said. "The Fierios left a message this morning." She tapped on her keyboard. "So that clears up a few hours. You've still got Guy Haskell's place, but you could do it alone. Doesn't he just want his kitchen and bathrooms done?"

"Yeah, and I could go this morning." Jazzy turned away from the bedroom and moved down the short hall and into the kitchen. Marbles sat on the counter, his gray eyes clearly saying, "Breakfast is late."

Jazzy bent to retrieve his bowls and washed them out. "Don't we have the Robertsons too? There's no way I can do their whole house myself." Well, she could, but the completely irrational side of her was actually considering Fabi's insane plea.

"I'll call them," Wren said. "See if we can reschedule for another time."

"The weekend," Jazzy said as she filled the water bowl and put it on the floor. She reached for the cat kibble. "I hate working weekends."

"I can come do it with you," Wren said. "It'll go quick."

Jazzy couldn't argue with that. Wren was an excellent maid, and Jazzy didn't get to spend much time with her now that she was married and had a little girl. She scooped cat food into the bowl and put it beside the water. Marbles jumped down from the counter, his striped tail held high, and padded over to his breakfast.

"So all I have on my schedule today is Guy's place." Plenty of time to get her hair done and even take Fabi's credit card and get herself something cute for a date that night.

I can't believe you're even considering this, she thought to herself. But she hadn't been out with a man in ninety-nine days, something she hadn't said to anyone, not even Fabi. And for some reason, Jazzy really didn't want to hit Day One Hundred.

"Yep, and give me five minutes to check with him and make sure you can come this morning instead of this afternoon. Then you can take care of Fabi the rest of the day."

Jazzy didn't have the heart to tell Wren that really she had time to get a new look in preparation for a date. Instead, she said, "Sure, five minutes," and hung up.

She immediate texted Starlee to find out if she had time to do a cut and color that day. The stylist's response came within seconds and said, *Absolutely. Tell me when.*

Jazzy had to wait to hear back from Wren, and when she did, she sent Starlee another text—*one o'clock?*—still in shock that she was actually considering going out with a man who'd only had eyes for her twin. Well, and his dogs, which Jazzy was sure was actually worse.

Chapter 2

Max Robinson tossed a weary look at the cockatiel squawking in the black iron cage sitting in the corner of his kitchen. Seeing the brightly colored bird always reminded him of his sister, Cathy, and his annoyance ebbed away.

Fifteen years younger than him, Cathy was the only girl in his family and she'd charmed him and his two younger brothers from the moment she was born. So when she'd gotten the bird her junior year of high school, they'd all accepted it. Then when she'd decided to cross state lines to go to college, Max had taken Birdy in.

Birdy.

He hated the name and disliked the bird most of the time. But Cathy loved it, and every time he called to ask her how her classes were going, or if she was dating anyone new, she asked about Birdy.

So he set his guitar gently on the floor and crossed over to the cage to feed Birdy. "You can't make so much noise while I'm gone," he told it, knowing the cockatiel would do whatever it wanted.

His next-door neighbor, an eighty-two-year-old widow who should probably be losing her hearing, never hesitated to tell him that the bird chattered constantly while he was at work. He'd tried covering the cage with a blanket, but that hadn't worked. No, Birdy was talkative and opinionated, and Max had learned to just smile and apologize to Matilda.

On his days off, he mowed her lawn and brought her pastries from the bakery. In the winter, he made sure her sidewalks and driveway were cleared of snow and salted. She made him dinner at least twice a week, and Max wasn't suffering from want of food or attention when it came to Matilda.

He fed Birdy and gave him fresh water before taking his guitar and moving to the back steps. Evening shade had started to creep across the grass, and he let his fingers pluck though whatever chords they wanted. A sense of nervousness plagued him, because tonight he was going out with Fabi Fuller. Finally.

He'd met her in Oxbow Park about two weeks ago, during one of his volunteer sessions with the local pet store. He was working with the dogs, throwing a couple of them balls while people walked around the safety fair. There had been five dog adoptions that day, and it had taken all of Max's willpower not to bring home the only remaining dog—a corgi that was blind in his right eye—himself.

He'd tried having a dog, but Birdy had gone berserk. So he'd resigned himself to being a cockatiel dad, a moonlighting guitar player, and the driver of one of two ambulances in Brush Creek.

Max drew in a big breath to calm himself. He'd been out with women before, but he'd sort of taken a break from dating over the past five years. Anyone who'd been in town for that long knew why, but Fabi hadn't seemed to know about Irina at all.

"That's because she's nine years younger than you," he said to himself, the guitar music still lilting in the background. He'd been married for a few years at age twenty-six, but Fabi hadn't had a serious boyfriend in years. There were some perks to living in a small town, and being able to ask around about one of the town's most familiar families was one of them.

Finally, it was time for him to get on over to Fabi's and pick her up. A measure of surprise pulled through him that she hadn't canceled, though her previous reasons had been valid.

He gripped the steering wheel with too much tension as he drove the few blocks to her apartment. She shared a place with her twin, and the pressure Max carried on his shoulders doubled. He wasn't sure if both women would be there, and he sort of hoped they wouldn't be. But

Jazzy wore her hair long, and at least Max could tell them apart.

He parked and made it up the steps to the second floor, feeling like a fifteen-year-old instead of a middle aged man. His pulse bumped around in his chest as he lifted his fist to knock. He only had to wait a few seconds before the gorgeous blonde whipped open the door and leaned her hip into it.

"Hey." She smiled in that magical way he'd seen at the park, her fingers curling around the side of the door. Her cute bob framed her face perfectly, making her blue eyes pop. Or maybe that was her bright red lipstick.

Max swallowed and told himself not to run his hand along his scalp. He'd gone bald at the age of eighteen and now just kept his head as hair-free as possible. Some women liked a bald man, but Max still had some self-consciousness about it, especially when faced with a woman who made his every male instinct come to life.

"Hey, yourself." He smiled. "I can't believe we're finally doing this."

She glanced over her shoulder as something sounded in the apartment behind her. Max searched for the source of the noise and found a gray tabby cat pawing his way across the carpet.

"Marbles," Fabi said in a condescending tone. She glanced back at Max, a glint of her own nerves in her eyes. "Give me a second, okay?" She dashed away, making her flared skirt sway and drawing Max's attention to her bare legs and pink-heeled feet.

He cleared his throat and looked away, unsure if he should go in or wait in the hall. He opted to wait in the hall as she swept the cat off the floor and took him out of sight. Female voices reached his ears, so her sister was clearly home, but Jazzy didn't come out.

Fabi appeared again, more pink in her cheeks that before. She pushed her breath out and reached for her purse. "Okay. I'm ready."

She joined him in the hall, and Max didn't give her much room to squeeze in beside him. A charge passed between them he hadn't experienced in the park, and she smelled like wildflowers and freshly washed cotton, also something he didn't remember. But they'd interacted for ten minutes, outside, with five dogs surrounding them. Max didn't want to think about what that smell had been.

"So, Clive's, right?" she asked, stepping toward the end of the hall where the stairs were.

Max put his hand lightly on the small of her back, the touch casual and innocent yet also sending a jolt through him. He pulled back, realizing he hadn't even made it out of the building before coming on too strong.

That was one thing he'd heard from the men around the fire and police departments. Fabi Fuller didn't want a man who came on too strong. She liked being in charge of the relationship. And here Max was, already touching her like it was his right.

"Right," he said. "Clive's. I think you said you liked the stuffed mushrooms."

Fabi stumbled, almost going head-first down the steps. Max grabbed her arm then, throwing caution to the wind as he slid his other hand around her waist to steady her. The last thing he needed was this date ending up with him driving her to the hospital. He did that all day, thank you very much. He didn't need to do it for the woman he'd been crushing on for weeks.

"Whoa," he said. She took a few seconds to find her feet, a nervous giggle filling the silence between them. "You okay?"

"Yeah. These heels are new." She stepped out of the circle of his help and took a slow, calculated step down. She made it safely to the bottom and flashed him a flirtatious look over her shoulder.

His cowboy boots made loud, echoing noises as he joined her in the lobby. "I like them." He hoped that was an appropriate compliment. Max couldn't believe how nervous he was, and he slicked his palms down his thighs before hurrying to step in front of Fabi so he could open the door for her.

She paused for a brief moment, her eyes meeting his with a sparkle of flirtation in them. "Thanks. I like your boots."

Max actually had to look down and see what he was wearing. His dark brown leather cowboy boots. As usual. Why his mind had gone so soft, he wasn't sure. He'd dated plenty of women over the years. He'd been married, for crying out loud.

By the time he got himself to function again, he realized Fabi was already walking around the front of his steel gray truck. He hurried to join her, opening that door for her too, hit with the crisp scent of the black ice air freshener he'd put in that morning. He didn't want her to know about his obsession with dill pickle sunflower seeds. At least Ed called it an obsession, and Max's partner in the ambulance knew him better than anyone else.

He joined Fabi in the truck and started the engine. After adjusting the dials to make the air conditioning at the right levels, he exhaled, some relief entering his muscles. "Hey, so this is kind of odd, but I have something to ask you." He glanced at her, the fear on her face a bit strange as well. She'd seemed fearless at the park a couple of weeks ago, and while she might be nervous about this first date, it didn't warrant the wash of horror in her bright eyes.

"You can say no," he added quickly, and that helped her relax. "So I've been talking to my partner about you and your sister, and he wondered if maybe Jazzy would want to go out with him. We could, you know, double. Or something."

Feeling like a fool, he forced himself to stop talking. She blinked rapidly a couple of times and looked away, out through her window. She clutched her purse in her lap like it was a snake that needed throttling.

Max had spent enough time on the job to see and feel tension in small ways. And Fabi was seriously anxious.

"Look," he said. "We don't have to go." He still

hadn't pulled out of the parking lot. She could go right back upstairs. He'd be disappointed, but she didn't seem all that keen on going out with him. Funny thing was, she'd seemed plenty interested at the park, and in all their subsequent communications. It was hard to feel emotion and get intent in a text, though. Max understood that better than most.

"Of course we're going to go," she said, her fingers releasing a little. "But I think I'll pass on the mushrooms. I haven't been feeling super great, and fungus doesn't sound appealing."

"We really can reschedule." He hoped she'd want that instead of just calling the whole thing off.

"No, no, it's fine." Her voice pitched up a notch. "My sister's had the flu, and I think maybe I'm getting a touch of it."

Max peered at her, glad when she graced him with a gorgeous smile. With his heart pounding, he said, "Maybe we should save Clive's for a time when you're feeling better."

"Yeah, maybe." She tilted her head and gave him a flirty look. "What about getting a smoothie and finding a quiet spot by the river? We can just talk."

Just talking sounded great to Max, and he relaxed a little bit more. "Sure. Do you want to go to Pick a Straw or Ruby's?"

"Pick a Straw. They have an amazing mango strawberry concoction that uses the local berries."

"Pick a Straw it is." Max pulled out and headed down

Main Street. Pick a Straw wasn't even a real shop, in a brick-and-mortar building, but a little hut on the side of the road. Max wouldn't even have paid it any attention if it wasn't for the dozen cars and long line of people in front of the bright red stand.

He pulled in, trying to act cool and casual that he was out with Fabi Fuller. *It's a first date*, he told himself. They weren't dating. She wasn't his girlfriend. He just wanted to get to know her better, maybe hold her hand on the next date, and kiss her down the line. At least he hoped that was the line they'd be following for a while.

She joined the line of people in front of Pick a Straw, her flared dress skimming the tops of her knees and making it clear she was on a date with Max. He stood maybe a fraction of an inch closer to her than was friendly for a first date, but she didn't move away.

"So did you take that corgi home?" she asked.

"Nah." He put his hands in his pockets. "I've got this bird I inherited from my sister, and she's all I can handle."

"A bird?"

"A cockatiel named Birdy."

She half-coughed, half-laughed. "Wow. Birdy. That's original."

Max chuckled too. "Right? My sister—she's awesome. I love her—but she doesn't always have the brightest ideas."

"Where is she?"

"Cathy's going to school in Denver. My parents

didn't want to keep the bird, and Cathy was in a fit about getting rid of it." Max shrugged, not really wanted to reveal this doormat side of himself so soon. "So I took it."

"Wow, what a great big brother." Fabi flashed him a smile and moved forward in line. "Other siblings?"

"Two brothers. The three of us are close in age. Ian is thirty-two. Rich is twenty-eight. Cathy is only twenty. She has us all wrapped around her little finger." He grinned, another shrug joining the conversation.

"And your family is in Vernal."

He'd mentioned that in the park. "My parents are. Rich lives there too and he's been dating the same girl for a couple of years now. My mother's dying for one of us to get married already, but Rich doesn't seem to want to be the first." Not that Rich would really be the first, but Max didn't correct himself.

No one in Max's family liked his girlfriend, and Max wasn't really sure why Rich hadn't broken up with Linnie or put a ring on her finger.

"So none of you are married?"

Max drew in a deep breath, not really prepared for all this talking. He'd assumed it would be surface stuff— favorite color, a movie that he loved. Not his family history and his entire romantic past.

"I was...once."

Surprise lifted Fabi's eyebrows and her eyes shone with curiosity. "Once?"

"Got married young. Didn't last too long. Been single for a while now."

"Any kids?"

"Nope."

"How young?"

"Twenty-six."

"How long?"

"Three years."

Fabi nodded, though more questions swam in her eyes. "What about you?" he asked, though he already knew. He'd been driving the ambulance in town for a decade—before Fabi had even graduated from high school. If she'd gotten married, he would've known. Everything the Fullers did was big town news, and they'd had a few weddings recently, so he knew.

Fabi tipped her head back and laughed. "No, sir. I've never been married." She sobered, but her smile remained. "Surely you know I hardly go on more than a first date."

Max indicated that she could move forward to hide his surprise. "I didn't know that." He stepped beside her, their turn at the hut coming up quick. "Why's that? Your choice or theirs?"

"I...." Silence hung between them, along with the sunshine and the smell of fruit and lemons and the chatter of other people surrounding them. She shrugged, her bare shoulders a sight that made Max's mouth water.

"Sometimes both," she said. "I...tend to act before I think. It's something I'm working on."

Max looked at her for a couple of heartbeats, glad he wasn't the only one making revelations today. "Fair enough." He put his hand on the small of her back and guided her forward again. She kept herself right beside him, their personal space mingling in a way that had Max's bones tingling.

He knew one thing: He wouldn't be the one to end things with her after only one date, and all he could do was pray that she'd go out with him a second time.

Chapter 3

Ed Moon glanced at the clock, trying to stuff his annoyance back inside a box inside himself. Max wasn't even late yet. Just because Ed had arrived forty minutes early—with doughnuts and coffee—didn't mean his partner had gotten the memo.

When Max finally entered the office, Ed took an extra second to glance up from his laptop, where he'd been surfing his social media accounts. He indicated the box of doughnuts, along with the to-go cup of coffee. "How was your date last night?"

"Amazing." Max sighed as he sat down, and Ed tried not to be jealous.

"I knew I should've taken that adopt-a-dog job." Ed grinned.

"Oh, come on." Max picked up the coffee cup and took a long draw.

"I knew I should've said yes to that instead of the first aid station," Ed said.

"You need a haircut." Max plucked an apple fritter from the box and bit into it, a playful look in his eyes.

Ed stroked his hand down the back of his head, realizing his hair was indeed so long it curled. He ran his fingers along his beard next. "Maybe I could get one of the Fuller twins to do it." He watched Max for a reaction, but his friend didn't give him one.

"I don't think they know how to cut hair," he said instead. "But hey, if you want, you could hire them to come clean your house."

"I thought you were going to ask Fabi about doubling."

"I did."

"And?" Ed looked back at his computer like he cared about the paperwork that needed filing. "The printer's on the fritz again."

Max grunted and took his time finishing his pastry. "I asked at the wrong time."

Ed speared Max with a look, not comforted when his friend wouldn't meet his gaze. "What does that mean?"

"It means I should've waited until I knew I'd have a second date before suggesting doubling."

Ed rolled his eyes. "You really are bad at this kind of stuff."

"Hey, I warned you." He pulled a folder closer to him and opened it, sipping his coffee as he scanned the document inside.

"So, will there be a second date?"

Max grinned like a wolf. "Tomorrow night."

"Why not tonight?" It was Friday—prime date night. If Max and Fabi had hit it off so well already, there had to be a reason for waiting an extra day.

"She said she couldn't." Max flipped the page in an annoyingly calm way. "I didn't ask for detailed specifics." He flicked Ed a look that said, *See? I'm not terrible at this kind of stuff.*

The conversation lulled between them, but Ed's mind didn't settle on the work he needed to do. Max seemed utterly nonplussed, and why shouldn't he be? He'd gone out with a beautiful woman, gotten a second date, and why wouldn't he? Just because he hadn't dated in a while didn't mean he was as rusty as he'd led Ed to believe.

Ed himself felt like the Tin Man, frozen in place, because he hadn't been out with someone remotely interesting in over a year. He'd been in Brush Creek for five, but it had taken him a while to get on the bus with Max. In small towns like this, the number of available spots were low, and people held onto them until retirement.

He knew it was a combination of luck and experience that had gotten him this job, and he was grateful for it.

"How's Maggie?" Max asked, breaking into Ed's thoughts. "Didn't she just start at the strawberry fields?"

"Yes, last week." Ed's jaw hardened. He hated that his sister had to work, but sometimes life dealt out impossible hands. "She says she likes it."

"Are you taking the girls to St. George this weekend?" Max flipped his phone over and around, something glinting in his eyes that annoyed Ed.

"I was going to, but I don't know if I'm up for the drive."

"Is Tad okay?"

"He's in one of his valleys." Ed didn't have to explain much more. He'd moved to Brush Creek five years ago when his sister's husband had been severely injured on the farm where he'd worked. He was disabled now, and that brought in a little bit of income. Maggie was a miracle-worker with money, and somehow she'd managed to stay home with their two girls until Charlene and Helen were in school full-time.

Tad was a good man who'd been given a bad situation, and honestly Ed felt like they were all doing the best they could. Ed took care of his sister's yard. He'd bought a house two doors down from hers. He took the girls in the evenings, on his days off, whenever he could. He took them to visit their grandparents in St. George, where he'd been born and raised. In short, he'd done everything he could to make life easier for his sister.

And he would continue to do so.

Max waved his phone. "I just got a text from Fabi. She says Jazzy's in for the movies tomorrow night if we want to double."

Ed's mind started whirring. He could take the girls all day, and see if Tad could handle them in the evening. Maggie spent weekends in Vernal, trying to get in enough hours in the salon to get her beautician license. She should be done by the end of the summer, and then she wouldn't have to be in the strawberry fields at four AM, but could open a salon in her house, where the girls could play in the room next door or the backyard while she worked.

"Give me ten minutes," Ed said, the hope of going out with someone ballooning in his chest in an relentless and totally unrealistic way.

———

Fabi added more blush to her cheeks. "He wants me to go out with Ed Moon?"

"Well, not you." Jazzy stood beside her at the double sink. "Technically, me. He wants *me* to go out with Ed and you to go out with him. Again." She threw Fabi a meaningful look. Maybe pointed, but everything Jazzy did was sharper than Fabi appreciated.

"When?"

"Tonight."

Fabi dropped her blush brush. "Tonight? Like... tonight?"

"That's why you're getting all dolled up." Jazzy flashed her a smile that whispered of revenge.

"You said we were going to the movies."

"We are."

"With Ed Moon and Max Robinson."

Jazzy pinned her bra strap to the inside of the shoulder strap of her dress. "That's right."

"So are we switching?"

Something akin to panic raced through Jazzy's expression. Fabi burst out laughing. "Oh my heck. You want to keep up the charade. You like Max Robinson."

Jazzy kept primping for a couple of seconds, then she turned to face her sister. "Yes, okay? I like him."

Fabi didn't know what to say. What to do. Her heart ping-ponged around in her chest. *She'd* been attracted to Max Robinson and the playful way he threw the ball to those dogs, yet had complete control over them.

"You were only supposed to hold my place for one date," she said, her voice on the outer edge of accusation.

Jazzy slumped against the counter. "I know." She threw her hands up in exasperation. "He's...charming. Sweet. Good-looking." Her features turned hard, covering her helplessness and reminding Fabi that Jazzy had always been the one to make the important decisions between them. Fabi liked to live by the seat of her pants, fly free, and let things go how they may. It was why she kissed too many men on the first date. Probably why she couldn't get a second one.

"He's interesting," Jazzy said. "And I haven't been out with anyone interesting in a long time."

Fabi's chest pinched again. Her sister didn't date even one-tenth as much as Fabi did, so not only had Jazzy not been out with anyone interesting in a while, she hadn't been on a date, period, in months.

Fabi should've never asked her to go out with Max in her place. It had been selfish and insensitive. And now Jazzy had made a connection with Max—and seemingly he had liked her too.

"Maybe this is how things were supposed to go," she said, defeat settling beneath her ribs. She hadn't even been out with Max. It was no real loss, though they had texted several times over the course of the past two weeks. He did seem charming and sweet. And he was good-looking.

"Did you act like me or you?"

"Just me," Jazzy said. "The only problem was I looked like you and answered to Fabi."

Fabi stepped next to Jazzy, and it really was remarkable how identical they looked. *On the outside*, Fabi reminded herself. But she and Jazzy really were their own people, and while she loved living with her sister, and spending time with her, and working together, sometimes she felt like half of a package. Like her by herself, she simply wasn't enough.

She stared into her own eyes, a brighter blue than Jazzy's, usually only noticeable if the two stood side-by-side, as they were now. Options ran through her mind, and she couldn't settle on one.

"Maybe we just try it," Jazzy suggested, her voice little more than a whisper. "Ed is very good-looking too."

Fabi cared less about looks and more about the charge between her and her date. And she'd felt something between her and Max—maybe just a small zing—at the park. Hadn't she? It had been so long ago, she wasn't sure.

"I haven't heard from Max at all," Fabi said. "How did you arrange all of this?"

"I told him I got a new phone that very afternoon."

"Jazzy." Fabi didn't mean for her voice to come out as a whine.

"I can name the last ten men you've been out with," Jazzy said. "In fact, I had to put Max off until tonight because you went out with Ronald Anniston last night. *Last night*, Fabi, you had yet another date with *another man*." Jazzy's whole body was animated now, and Fabi squirmed under the weight of her sky-blue gaze.

"Good thing that flu was only a twenty-four-hour thing," Fabi offered feebly.

Jazzy didn't flinch, but gazed unwaveringly at her sister. "Can you even name one man I've been out with in the past—let's say a year. I'll give you *a year* to name someone I've been out with."

Fabi met her sister's eyes, so full of challenge and fire, already wilted. "Do you have a picture of Ed?"

CHAPTER 4

J azzy was just as nervous on her second date with Max as she had been on the first. This time, her anxiety was borne from an entirely different reason. Guilt squirmed through her that she was lying to him, because she really did like him. If their relationship were to go somewhere, she'd have to tell him. She couldn't be Fabi forever. Could she?

Of course not, she told herself as the doorbell rang. Fabi twisted from where she was putting the breakfast bowls into the dishwasher, barely a glance at the door. She'd been picked up so many times, it was probably second-nature to her to take a few extra seconds to finish her chore.

Then she washed her hands. Then she smoothed down the long pieces of hair framing her face and practically flounced over to the door. She opened it about two feet, not nearly enough for Jazzy to see who stood in the hall, and said, "Well, hello, boys," in a tone that made Jazzy cringe.

She was supposed to be the flirty one. She hurried forward and said, "Jazzy," in a very stern voice.

Fabi looked at her with widening eyes. "Oh—" The rest of her sentence came out in a squeak.

Jazzy looked at Max—big, broad, and beautiful—standing in the hall, covering his baldness with a ball cap, wearing a gray T-shirt that said "Suck it up, Buttercup," and a delicious pair of dark jeans. He'd brought along the cowboy boots again, and he made Jazzy want to be as country as possible.

Beside him stood the dark-haired, bearded, in-the-flesh version of the picture Max had sent her that morning. Ed had a square jaw and full lips, and ebony eyes that seemed to be devouring both Fabi and Jazzy.

"I'm Fabi," Jazzy said, extending her hand to Ed. "You must be Max's bus partner."

Max choke-laughed.

"Hey, I tried." Jazzy giggled with a shrug. "It does sound cooler when you say it."

"Bus partner." Max gestured to Ed, standing there in brown loafers, a pressed pair of khaki pants, and a blue striped polo. "Ed Moon. Fabi." He switched his gaze to the actual Fabi. "And her twin sister, Jazzy."

Both men volleyed their gazes between the twins, something both Fabi and Jazzy were used to after twenty-seven years of it.

"My eyes are darker," Fabi said, giving them a way to

tell them apart. She scanned Jazzy's blue, teal, red, and yellow striped dress. "And I would never wear stripes."

Max blinked and then looked at Ed's shirt. "Bad choice, buddy."

Fabi physically startled, and Jazzy started laughing. This was much more than a giggle, but she couldn't help herself. Fabi was always the one in charge, the one making the quips, the one drawing all the male eyes. It was actually refreshing to see her struggle a little bit.

Her face filled with a flush. "I mean—" she stammered, finally pressing her lips closed and looking at Jazzy with helplessness in her darker blue eyes.

"She likes stripes fine," Jazzy said. "Just not on her. Thinks they make her look fat." She whispered the last word and reached for her purse on the table by the door. Fabi wore a little black dress tonight, her usually fare for a weekend date. She owned so many little black dresses, Jazzy had stopped counting at eight. In fact, this ribbed, textured outfit was new.

"Some of us like color." Jazzy flashed Ed a smile as she joined the men in the hall. "I think your shirt is great."

"I do too," Fabi said, stepping outside and pulling the door closed behind her. "Really, I do."

Jazzy caught Ed's quick nod, his playful smile, before she moved with Max as they went first down the hall to the steps. Electricity crackled between her and Max, and a blip of a thought beat through her.

Tell him. Tell him.

You can't tell him. You can't tell him.

She'd literally just let him introduce her to his best friend as Fabi. Her stomach jumped all over the place, creating a well of anxiety that no amount of buttered popcorn would be able to soothe.

Behind her, Fabi made small talk with the ease of breathing, but Jazzy literally could not think of a single thing to say. During her date on Thursday, she'd managed just fine, and she hoped she hadn't used up all available conversation topics in one night.

"What do you guys do if a call comes in?" she asked as he held open the door for her.

"What do you mean?"

"Well, you're both off tonight. What if an emergency call comes in?"

"There are eight paramedics in Brush Creek," Ed answered. "We rotate shifts and have some days off."

"So you won't have to run out of the movie." Jazzy smiled at Max's best friend. She could see why the men got along so well. Their eyes met for a moment and Max grinned.

"Depends on if it's a big accident or not."

"Do we get a lot of big accidents?" Fabi asked. "I can't even remember the last time I even heard a siren in town."

"Sure," Ed said, guiding Fabi around to the back of a white sedan. "The big accidents happen on the highway between here and Vernal."

"He's right," Max said. "I've seen them lots of times when I drive back and forth."

"Max is from Vernal," Jazzy said. Fabi nodded and ducked into the backseat. She got in the car too, and Max closed her door. The air was stuffy, hot from the early June sunlight shining through the windows. It smelled like fabricated air freshener, and Jazzy spotted the orange tree around the gear shift.

The two men walked around the front of the car, taking their sweet time. Which was just fine with Jazzy, because it gave her enough time to say, "We have to tell them," to Fabi.

"How do you propose to do that?" her sister asked.

Jazzy flipped down the sunshade and opened the mirror, pretending to check her lip gloss. Really, she met her sister's eye. "Maybe you'll break up with Ed tomorrow, but I like Max."

"Fine." Fabi folded her arms and gave Jazzy a death glare. "Tell him."

The door opened in the next instant, and the men slid into their seats. "Are we ready?" Max asked, cutting a glance at Jazzy. He almost looked away, but then focused his eyes on hers. "You okay?"

She half nodded and half shook her head no. She wasn't sure how she felt, and she couldn't get any words to cross her vocal chords anyway.

In the back seat, Ed said something about chicken sandwiches, and Fabi's shrill voice exclaiming her love of the criss-cross fries that came with the meal silenced anything Jazzy might've blurted. Max held her gaze for another moment before Ed tapped his shoulder and said, "We have time to eat, right?"

"Sure." Max chuckled and pulled out of the apartment parking lot.

Fabi was exceptional at small talk, and asking questions, and Jazzy let her fill the car with chatter and laughter. No wonder she always enjoyed her first dates. She liked talking about herself and she liked asking other people about themselves.

Though they only drove maybe a mile to Chicken House, by the time Jazzy got out of the car, the silence was welcome. Max caught her eye, and a silent understanding passed between them, along with another zip of that attraction that had her heart bobbing in the back of her throat.

"So are you as excited about these chicken sandwiches as I am?" he asked as he met her at the front of the car. He tossed a sarcastic smirk to Ed.

"Hey," his friend said. "I've seen you eat three in one sitting."

"I'm sure that's not true." Max shifted his feet, and Jazzy thought it absolutely was true. She turned toward the front of the fast food restaurant that did make killer chicken sandwiches. She loved the mustard-mayo combination that was just the right amount of tangy against the hot, fried chicken.

The evening held the summer heat, and the temperature took a severe upswing when Max brushed her fingers with his. A breath of touch. There, then gone. She jerked her attention toward him, caught his shy smile, and tried to contain her giddiness when he slipped his hand into hers on the next step.

Jazzy seriously could not remember the last time she'd held hands with a man. Especially one as good-looking, charming, and kind-hearted as Max. He asked her about Kyler, because she'd told him a couple of days ago that her brother had been sick.

She could barely remember her own name, but she managed to answer with, "I took him some soup last night. He seemed a little better."

"Dahlia's out on a case, right?"

"That's right." Jazzy paused behind Fabi and Ed, who seemed to be listening to their conversation. "Kyler seemed grateful for the company."

"Dahlia's good people," Ed said. "We've worked with her on cases before."

"Oh?" Jazzy glanced at him and found his focus on her and Max's joined hands. Fabi's gaze fell there too, and a squeak of surprise escaped her lips. Jazzy lifted her chin, daring her sister to make another noise. "Why would you work with a detective?"

"If they want medical records, interviews, patient awareness during transport. That kind of stuff." Ed stepped forward, and Max squeezed her hand when they didn't have more attention on them.

She met his eye and squeezed back. He didn't seem like the type to date-and-dump, and a tingle of joy tangled with Jazzy's other emotions inside. She'd have to tell him who she really was eventually, but for now, he seemed to only have eyes for her and that sure was nice.

———

ED HAD KNOWN his buddy had really enjoyed himself with Fabi Fuller on Thursday night. The way his phone had chimed incessantly on Friday had been the tip of the iceberg. Because now Max was holding hands with her, right there in Chicken House, where anyone could see them.

Max never was one to be too public with his affections. Irina had squashed that right out of him, then left town before the divorce papers had even been served. Ed had only been in town for a couple of months when it all went down, and it was like headline news for a few weeks until the drama shifted to something else.

In fact, Max hadn't dated much at all in the five years since his first marriage ended. But he seemed to really like Fabi, and the way she crowded close to him in her bright green heels testified that she liked him too.

Ed cast a glance at Jazzy. She was gorgeous, no doubt about that. Quieter than he'd expected, though he knew the fun, flirty twin currently held hands with his best friend. Ed didn't mind the more subdued blonde, and the fact that she ordered her chicken sandwich with extra pickles only endeared her more to him.

"Extra pickles, huh?" he asked.

"Oh, yeah. I love pickles." She flashed him a smile full of straight, white teeth. "Don't tell me you're one of those men who doesn't like pickles on hamburgers."

"They do tend to take over the whole sandwich." He looked at the cashier and put in his own order. "*Two* chicken sandwiches with extra pickles and criss-cross fries with frozen lemonade."

He grinned at her as he stepped to her side so Max and Fabi could order. "But I like 'em just fine."

"My brothers won't eat them," she said. "Kyler throws a fit about warm pickles." She giggled, a pretty little sound that wormed its way into Ed's heart.

"My sister is pretty picky too," he said.

"How many siblings do you have?" Jazzy asked.

"Just Maggie," he said. "She's why I moved here. Her husband got hurt, and they needed help."

"Maggie Wainwright?"

Ed met those darker blue eyes and had to coach himself not to dive in too soon. "Yeah. You know her?"

"Of course I know her," she said. "She works for us in a pinch."

"Who does?" Fabi asked, having placed her order.

"Maggie." Jazzy thumbed her finger at Ed. "That's his sister." She gave him a full-on smile that only said flirt. "If I'd have known she had a handsome, available older brother, I would've pried a bit more into her life."

"Oh, so I'm handsome now? The stripes don't repulse you?" He grinned as he spoke, glad when she tipped her head back and laughed. She had a slender neck

Ed wanted to touch with his lips, and he cleared his throat, his grin fading fast.

What kind of thought was that?

Inappropriate, he told himself. He barely knew this woman, and he wouldn't operate on purely physical attraction. Not again. Not anymore.

Their food came quickly, as it always did at Chicken House, and Ed let Max take the lead while he tried to figure out what kind of spark there was between him and Jazzy.

Because it was definitely there. Hot and spiraling, almost like those ground flower fireworks Maggie's girls loved so much. He met her eye, and Jazzy ducked her head, the longer pieces of her hair falling between them.

Feeling brave and bold, Ed reached up and pushed them back. He balanced their food in one hand while everything around them fell away. Her dark blue eyes molded to his dark brown ones, and he saw more there than she probably wanted to admit.

He dropped his hand and slid into the booth beside Max, who had fixed him with a cautious look. "Don't feel like you need to wolf it down," he said. "But we do need to leave for the movies in twenty minutes."

"Can we get popcorn there?" Fabi asked.

"After dinner?" Jazzy asked her sister, her eyebrows high. She plucked one criss-cross fry form her cardboard container and bit off a tiny piece. Ed really didn't want her to be the kind of woman who didn't eat on dates.

"Sure," Max said at the same time Fabi said, "It's not a movie if there's no popcorn," and shrugged.

Ed was definitely in Fabi's camp on this one, but he still managed to eat all of his food. Jazzy, thankfully, did too. They arrived at the theater and joined the line to get their popcorn with extra butter, making it to their seats just as the previews started.

Ed relaxed in the dark. For some reason, he felt very much under the microscope with Jazzy. She was smart, obviously, and funny, and so pretty it almost hurt to look at her. Why Ed had never seen her before he wasn't entirely sure. The Fullers were a well-known family in Brush Creek, and surely the twins had been at most of the social events in town.

The movie started, and not ten minutes had gone by before Jazzy lifted the armrest between them. "Do you mind?" she whispered.

Ed certainly did not mind. He lifted his arm over her shoulders as she cuddled into his side, sighing as if cradled against his chest was exactly where she wanted to be. He felt like someone had poured jumping beans into his blood, and he worked to keep from twitching.

Jazzy smelled like tropical fruit and sunshine, both items Ed needed more in his life. If the rumors he'd heard since yesterday could be trusted, she didn't date nearly as much as her sister. But she certainly didn't seem out of practice.

It was Fabi who was supposedly forward, but Jazzy had practically climbed into his lap within an hour of meeting him. A smile curved his lips. He liked this woman and the gentle pressure of her body against his. Now, he couldn't say if he liked the movie or not, because he barely watched a minute of it after Jazzy snuggled in to his side. And somehow, it was the best money he'd ever spent.

CHAPTER 5

Fabi knew she shouldn't have lifted the arm rest between her and Ed. Jazzy had given her a wide-eyed glare that she'd deserved. At the same time, she couldn't help it. Ed obviously spent a lot of time in the gym when he wasn't riding shotgun in the ambulance. He smelled like soap and something woodsy, and Fabi had no defense against a man who smelled as good as he did.

He obviously hadn't minded either, if the way his fingers traced an unknown pattern on her upper arm was any indication.

At home now, she stared up at the ceiling above her bed, wondering how she could tell him who she really was. Because though she'd only been out with him once, they'd exchanged phone numbers and he'd finally stopped texting her about ten minutes ago.

Jazzy had fallen asleep at least an hour ago, and Fabi

stared into the dark silence, knowing that she wanted to keep dating Ed the same way Jazzy wanted to go out with Max again.

She closed her eyes, her fantasies of tracing her fingers down his jaw, his beard tickling her skin, bringing a smile to her face. She hadn't kissed a man with a beard in a while.

"And you're not kissing him for weeks," she whispered to herself. Instantly, an internal war began, but the rational part of Fabi argued against rushing into things, scaring Ed off, and causing undue problems for herself.

When she woke the following morning, she was still no closer to a solution for how to get her and Jazzy with the right men, under the right names.

"We have to do something," she told Jazzy as she came into the bathroom bleary-eyed.

"Yeah, sure," she mumbled. "I'm showering. Can we do something after that?"

Fabi finished rinsing her teeth and left her sister alone in the bathroom. She dressed in a pale yellow dress with a brown leather belt, wondering if the paramedic partners attended church. It was expected as a Fuller, and Fabi had never really minded. Sure, she'd gone through a year or two right after leaving her parents' house where she slept in and skipped church, or drove to Vernal and hiked up to the hieroglyphs instead of listening to a sermon.

But she'd come back, because she liked the hour where she got to sit and do nothing. Sit and think. Sit and feel like there was more to her life than furniture polish and disinfectant wipes. At least she certainly hoped there was more for her than the family cleaning business.

She and Jazzy had been cleaning houses since they'd turned fourteen years old. Always side-by-side, always splitting the income and tips fifty-fifty. Neither of them had any inclination to go to college, and they both liked their work. In fact, the only reason Fabi had even considered leaving town was to find a bigger dating pond to fish from.

She sat at her vanity and put on her makeup, taking extra care to get the wing on her eyeliner precisely right. Jazzy came in and dressed, did her makeup, and fixed her hair before Fabi stood from her dressing table.

Jazzy stood in the kitchen, a rubber spatula working the liquid eggs into scrambled solids. "Breakfast?"

"Yeah. And we need to talk about setting things right with Ed and Max."

Jazzy cut her a glare and scooped half the eggs onto one plate, and the other half onto another. She set the syrup between them and came around to sit beside Fabi at the bar.

"How are we going to do that?"

"I don't know, but it has to be done."

"You like Ed." Jazzy took a bite of her eggs. "Either that, or you just wanted to put on a show last night."

"I did not put on a show." Fabi drizzled maple syrup in diagonal lines across her scrambled eggs.

"Oh, please." Jazzy snorted and scoffed. "Poor Mrs. Hoffman almost went and got an usher."

"She did not." Fabi rolled her eyes though her cheeks heated slightly. Maybe she had put on a bit of a show. But it wouldn't be a date without a little bit of drama. "Besides, Ed didn't seem to mind."

"Of course he didn't." Jazzy shook her head. "You...*I* don't act like that."

"I'm not you."

"But he thinks you are."

"It's not like we've met before."

Jazzy shook her head again, her lips practically disappearing into a thin line while she chewed.

"What?" Fabi asked.

"You're delusional if you think they haven't done their homework on us." She got up, though she hadn't finished eating, and put her plate in the sink. "We're Fullers. They know everything about us."

"You think so?"

"I know so." Jazzy opened the shoe closet and selected a pair of black heels. "Come on. We're going to be late for church."

Fabi left her plate on the counter and slipped into a pair of wedge booties. "You really think they asked around about us?" she asked as they exited the building. For some reason, the idea bothered her.

"Well, Tate works in the same building as they do. Dahlia too, when she's in town. And that's easy access to Wren and Kyler. So do I think Ed and Max have asked about us?" Jazzy hogged the half of the sidewalk that was bathed in shade. "Of course they have."

Fabi fell silent and let the breeze and Jazzy's heels make all the noise as they passed the bakery and started across the parking lot toward the red brick church.

"I'll hold back," Fabi said as they neared the doors.

"Why would you do that?" Jazzy looked at her, which made Fabi sweat more than the June heat usually merited.

Fabi had the distinct impression that Jazzy already knew why, but she wanted Fabi to say it out loud. She reached for the door handle, the blast of air conditioning pushing her hair away from her face.

"I like Ed, and I want to go out with him more than once." She started to step through the door, but Jazzy touched her arm and made her pause.

"More than twice?" she asked.

Fabi's pulse raced around her body, and she searched her sister's face. Of course, Jazzy knew that Fabi hadn't been out with anyone more than twice in a long time. In fact, there had only been a few men that Fabi had wanted to go out with more than twice.

And Ed was one of them.

She grinned and said, "Yeah, I want to go out with him more than twice."

———

"Gotta call outside of Maple Mountain." Max knocked on the desk as he shrugged into his paramedic vest.

He swiped the keys to the ambulance off the hook on the wall, not bothering to see if Ed was following him. Of course he was. He'd seen the flashing red stripe on his computer too. Max had clicked forward, and the address would be waiting on the GPS console in the bus.

"I don't want to say I'm thankful," Ed said as he buckled his seatbelt. "But I wasn't sure I could sit there for another day, pushing paper."

"I hear you." Max had a love-hate relationship with his job. He loved being able to help people. He loved that he knew how to stop bleeding on a head wound and that he didn't panic at the sight of blood and other bodily fluids. That alone had helped him through a lot of stressful situations with his first wife.

But the desk aspect of the job was not something he favored. Even getting paid to go to the gym seemed ridiculous when he was there for half of his shift. Plus, muscles needed time to rebuild before he could tear them down again.

He didn't like that someone needed their services, but this call seemed like a legitimate accident, not someone's cat that had gotten stuck in a tree or a schnauzer trapped on a barn roof. He'd saved that silly Cupcake more than he wanted to admit—and in his opinion a dog should never be named Cupcake.

"It's been a long week," Ed said, rolling his neck as

Max set the ambulance north and hit the switches to get the sirens and lights going.

"Only because you haven't been able to see Jazzy," he teased. Though Fabi had likewise been "busy," Max had hidden his emotions better than Ed.

"No," Ed said quickly.

"When are you goin' out with her again?" Max loved the thrill of driving fast, lights on, siren blaring. Of course, in the middle of the day, there wasn't much traffic to contend with, especially once they rushed past the strawberry fields.

"Saturday night."

"Ah, you got yourself another date." Max grinned at his friend.

"Yep. And you're comin' to help me move some things for Maggie that morning, remember?"

"I remember."

"When are you seeing Fabi again?"

"Tonight. She texted this morning." Neither twin had mentioned doubling again, and Ed and Max had talked about the situation at length. In the end, they'd decided to let the women set the pace, lead the way, dictate the dates.

"What are you doing?"

"She said she wanted to get outside her comfort zone."

"Does Fabi Fuller have a comfort zone? I thought she was the adventurous one."

"She said she's lived in the country her whole life and

never taken up horseback riding. I guess we're goin' up to the canyon to the horse farm. Her brother-in-law has a horse boarded there and says the riding instructors are great."

Ed pinned him with a look. "Do you ride horses?"

Max threw a handful of pickle-flavored sunflower seeds in his mouth, his taste buds puckering at the sourness. "Sure. Vernal's a big horse town." At least Max hoped riding a horse was like riding a bike, because he hadn't done it in several years. But how hard could it be?

They came upon the accident and all small talk ceased. Ed got out the stretcher while Max shouldered his medical bag. Two cars were smashed up, and a woman sat in the driver's seat of the black sedan, her door open, one leg out. She seemed awake, at least.

McDermott, the state trooper in these parts, approached. "Head-on collision when the driver of the blue SUV fell asleep and crossed the center line." He hooked his thumb over his shoulder to the black sedan. "She was traveling east at the time."

Her car wasn't facing east anymore, and Max nodded. "Did she lose consciousness?"

"That's unclear. The driver of the SUV made the nine-one-one call."

"Where's he?" Ed asked.

"Lying down in his vehicle." McDermott's mouth pinched into a tight line. "He's complaining of headaches, chest pains, and he's got some nasty burns on his arms from the air bag."

"I'll take him," Ed said. "You take the woman."

Max nodded his thanks to McDermott and approached the black sedan. He took one deep breath and pushed it out slowly. Again, and then again before crouching down and letting his heavy medical bag rest on the ground.

"Ma'am?" The fact that she didn't turn at his approach concerned him. "My name's Max. How about you tell me what hurts?"

She swung her head in his direction, and she looked dazed. She blinked slowly, almost like it was happening in slow motion. She said nothing, and while Max recognized her, he couldn't place her name in his mind.

"Can you tell me your name?" He reached for his stethoscope, making careful, measured movements to unzip his bag.

"Winnie," she said, her voice croaky and soft.

"That's right." Max smiled at her and placed his device against her chest. "I'm just going to listen here for a minute, okay, Miss Winnie?" He focused on the ground as he listened to her pulse. "Sounds okay."

He scanned her from foot to head, finding several small burns, cuts, and abrasions. "What's your last name?"

Max had placed her as Winnie Towers, and when she said it, he smiled. "You've got a big bump on your head here." He touched the spot just above her left eye and probed back into her hair. "What did you hit your head on?"

"The window?" Winnie made it sound like a guess.

"Have you called anyone?" He didn't need to glance at the hood of the car to know it was totaled. The smell of various liquids leaking from it and the quick scope he'd taken when he'd arrived was enough.

"I live alone," the older woman said. "I have a son in Vernal."

Max's heart twisted the tiniest bit. "I think you should go to the hospital; get some scans. I can call your son for you."

"All right."

"Do you think you can stand?"

She put her weight on one foot but made no attempt to get out of the car.

"Okay," Max said in his kindest voice. "Stay put. Let me go talk to the trooper, and we'll get you the help you need." The bus would be needed for the man Ed was currently strapping to the stretcher. But Winnie needed transportation to the hospital too, that much was clear.

As he walked over to McDermott to make the arrangements, he also vowed to call his parents that night. After all, he hadn't spoken to them in a couple of weeks and he'd want them to know to call him if they were ever in Winnie's situation.

———

I'M fifteen minutes behind schedule. Max sent the text to Fabi as soon as he stepped inside his apartment, the accident up at Maple Mountain taking much longer to sort through than he'd anticipated. He hurried into the shower, his stomach growling, and he tossed some food at Birdy before darting back out to the carport.

He showed up at Oxbow Park, only twelve minutes later than he and Fabi had agreed, to find her leaning against the black iron fence. She gazed out over the water, a look of peace on her face that had Max wishing he was with her wherever she'd gone inside her mind.

"Hey," he said, stepping beside her.

She blinked and a smile lit up her whole face. "Hey, you made it."

"Busy afternoon." He put the accident and the way Winnie reminded him of his mother out of his mind. He'd learned to compartmentalize during his medical training. He could apply it to real life too. "You look real nice."

She wore a pair of jean shorts that went halfway down her thighs and a silky blouse the color of the lilac bush in his backyard. She glanced at herself, an inkling of surprise in her eyes. Max couldn't take his eyes off of her, and his thoughts ran rampant. What would it be like to kiss her? Could he ever see himself falling in love again? Getting married?

When everything had broken with Irina, Max had vowed to keep his heart inside a safe box, make sure it didn't get so shattered again.

But the intensity between him and Fabi was a force that couldn't be denied, and he thought maybe he'd endure any number of cracks in his heart if he got to spend more time with her.

He'd held her hand last weekend, and his fingers had been reminding him about it for days. When he finally slipped his between hers again, a sigh passed through his whole body. "Are we walking?"

She'd suggested they meet at the park, but she hadn't said why. This wasn't the horse farm, and as far as he could tell, there were no horses here at all. But the water was calm, almost a mirror for the trees and blue sky above, and a measure of that peace he'd seen on her face pulled through him too.

"I love this place," she said, a wistful quality in her voice. She didn't move to walk along the paved trail that led around the lake.

"I do too."

She seemed a bit lost inside herself, and Max didn't try to pull her out. She finally drew in a long breath, her chest lifting with the effort.

"Hey, you okay?" he asked.

She met his gaze with seven shades of fear in hers. "No."

Max swallowed, sure she was about to break up with him after only two dates. He searched his mind for what he'd done wrong. He hadn't kept her up too late with texts. He'd tried not to come on too strong with his questions.

"What's goin' on?" he asked when she still didn't speak.

Her hand tightened against his. "I have something to tell you, and I want you to promise you won't be mad."

Max frowned, way past the age where he promised such things. "I don't know, Fabi...."

"I'm not Fabi," she blurted, her cornflower blue eyes widening as tears filled them.

He shook his head, sure he'd heard her wrong. "What?"

She drew herself up and a sharp edge entered her eyes now. "I'm not Fabi."

CHAPTER 6

J azzy watched the confusion sweep across Max's handsome face. That cute little frown stayed, pulling his eyebrows down, and she sucked back the urge to babble the truth in nonsensical sentences.

"I really like you," she said instead. "And it was just a big misunderstanding, but I didn't want it to continue."

He opened his mouth to say something, but promptly closed it again.

"Do you want the whole story?" she asked, somewhat encouraged that he hadn't ripped his hand away from hers yet.

"I think so, yeah." He glanced around like he couldn't believe what he was seeing.

"So you met the real Fabi in the park a few weeks ago. That was her."

Max's eyes came right back to hers. "Really?"

Jazzy hated that he hadn't even known her hair had been different that day he'd met Fabi. She nodded though a sliver of ice moved through her bloodstream.

"Yeah, it was her. She does have the darker eyes. And the mole on the side of her jaw. And the A-line cut. I didn't have any of those things."

Max appraised her now, his gaze turning more and more knowledgeable. She pulled her hand out of his, her chest so tight, so tight.

"But she had a hard time getting together with you, and she didn't want to break your date again last week."

"Why would she have to?" His voice sounded like he'd scraped his throat with sandpaper.

"She had the flu." Jazzy tossed him a miserable look. "So she begged me to get my hair cut and meet you. I—" She could not get herself to tell this beautiful man that she hadn't been out with anyone in so long, and how desperate she was for a little bit of attention, so she just shook her head.

"You said yes. You pretended to be her." At least he could put the pieces together without her having to spell everything out.

"Yeah." She gazed out over the lake, which she'd always loved. She hoped this would not be the place where she lost her chance with Max Robinson. "I'm sorry. I wanted to tell you. I gave you my phone number, so we've been texting since our date last week. I was going to tell you. Then you suggested that Ed go out with Jazzy, and well...things just got out of control."

Her pulse quieted slightly now that she'd spilled the truth. Fabi would be livid, but Jazzy had vowed not to go on another date with Max when he didn't know who she was.

The warmth from his body seeped into her side as he settled his weight against the fence, much too close to her to be casual. They breathed in together, then out, and then Max slid his arm around her, slowly. So slowly, Jazzy had several long, delicious moments to savor the feel of his strong hand along her lower back.

"You know what?" he said, his voice low and dripping with honey.

"What?" Jazzy didn't dare look at him, hoping he didn't hug all the women he broke up with.

"I don't care," he said. "I don't care that you pretended. I...." He cleared his throat, and Jazzy dared to take a peek at him. He stared out over the water too, a muscle in his jaw jumping.

"I like you too," he said. "*You*. Whether your name is Fabi or Jazzy." He turned and looked at her, their eyes locking. For the first time in her life, Jazzy felt like someone was looking right at her and not flicking their eyes to Fabi to see which sister it was, which twin they were more interested in.

Because inevitably, it was always Fabi.

But not this time.

Jazzy could hardly believe it, but looking into Max's penetrating blue eyes, it seemed that his interest was in her alone.

A smile tugged at the corners of her mouth. "My name is Jazzy. I used to have long hair and my eyes are lighter than my sister's. Oh, and I actually like dogs." She lifted her eyebrows and half-shrugged.

Max let a beat of silence go by before he chuckled. He kneaded her closer and said, "I think you wanted to ride horses tonight. Are we still doing that?"

Jazzy wasn't sure why she'd been so worried about telling him, but Fabi had insisted that they shouldn't. Even though both twins had agreed not to go out with their respective men again until they could figure out a solution, Jazzy had learned that morning that Fabi had set a date with Ed for Saturday night.

Since they hadn't agreed on anything, Jazzy had asked her sister what the plan was.

"Nothing," Fabi had said.

Nothing. The word still rang in Jazzy's head. Her sister was planning on continuing the ruse with Ed, and that had made Jazzy's blood boil. Sometimes she really disliked Fabi's devil-may-care attitude.

So she'd texted Max and then determined to tell him before they went up to the horse farm.

"So, do you want to drive?" he asked as they started toward the parking lot.

"You can."

"I, uh, didn't bring my truck." He stopped next to a shiny, black motorcycle and grinned.

Jazzy's stomach fell to the ground and then pinged back into place. "Oh, uh."

Fabi had told her once about riding a motorcycle with one of her dates. Tom...something. He'd worn a leather jacket and sunglasses and Fabi had found him dangerous and sweet at the same time.

"I can drive your car," Max suggested.

"No," Jazzy said, making a snap decision. "I want to ride this with you." She looked at the smallness of the seat and tried to ignore the fact that she wasn't wearing proper footwear. Wren had told her the cowboys would have boots up at the ranch, that she didn't need any special gear. How could she have known that she'd need closed-toed shoes for the ride up to the ranch?

"Do you have an extra helmet?" she asked, half hoping he didn't.

"As a matter of fact." He reached for the saddlebags on the back of the bike. "I do." He pulled out a bright red helmet and handed it to her.

She pulled it over the haircut she hated and thrilled when his warm fingers touched her chin as he helped her buckle it in place.

Max ducked his head, a hint of shyness in his eyes that endeared him to Jazzy even more. Without thinking, she reached out and ran her fingertips along the top of his skull. It was smooth and beautiful and she curled her fingers around his earlobe as his heated gaze met hers.

She flinched and dropped her hand. "I—I'm sorry."

Max put a few extra feet of distance between them and pulled on his own helmet. "Nothing to be sorry about." He swung his leg over the seat and added, "Climb on, Jazzy."

Hearing her name in his round, bass voice brought another grin to her face, and she joined him on the motorcycle, the hum of it underneath her nearly as thrilling as wrapping her arms around the very solid mass of a man in front of her.

Who was she kidding? Max was really who got her heartbeat thrumming and her mind dancing through fantasies, not some silly motorcycle. But the bike certainly added to his allure, and Jazzy liked the entire package.

A man named Walker Thompson met her and Max in the stables, and two more cowboys arrived very soon after initial introductions were made.

"Emmett," Walker said. "And Ted. They'll help you two get your horses and get started tonight." Walker smiled and headed out, and somehow the thought of getting on a horse while these three men watched her had Jazzy's stomach in triple knots.

But then Max replaced his ball cap with a cowboy hat, and Jazzy's whole world tilted in a very good way.

ED GOT out of his car after parking behind Max's motorcycle. His partner sat on the front steps of Maggie's house, a black cat at his side.

"What's with you and stray animals?" Ed laughed as he came closer.

Max reached down and patted the cat, which hissed and streaked away, probably because Ed was a lot less forgiving than Max when it came to strays.

He tossed a bag of dill pickle-flavored sunflower seeds to his friend. "Thanks for coming to help."

Max caught the bag against his chest, surprise in his eyes. "Maggie's feeding us lunch, right? Because if she's not making that sausage and pepper Alfredo pizza, I'm walkin' out right now."

Ed chuckled. "You have a thing for food too."

"Hey, I'm not great in the kitchen, and your sister is."

"How was the horseback riding?"

Max's neck turned a ruddy shade of red. "Uh, it was okay."

Ed kept a close eye on his best friend. "What happened?"

"So apparently it's not as easy as it was when I was in high school."

Ed chuckled and shook his head. "Few things are, my friend. I hope you didn't hurt yourself, because we're moving beds today."

"I can handle a couple of beds."

Ed stood and nudged Max with his foot, watching as the other man got to his feet a little gingerly. "Did you fall off a horse or something?"

"I'm fine."

"Whatever." Ed almost started laughing at the

thought of the mighty Max Robinson making a fool of himself with a horse in front of Fabi. "Let's hope Tad's doing okay today." Ed had done more than hope; he'd been praying for a few days now.

He knocked on the door and pushed it open. "Hello?" He stepped inside, aware that Max had followed him with a slight groan pulling through his throat.

High-pitched squeals met his ears and two little girls barreled around the corner, their arms waving as they ran toward him. Ed braced himself as Charlene flung herself into his arms. "Uncle Ed, you're here!" The five-year-old weighed next to nothing, as if she were made of smiles and sunshine, and Ed laughed as she touched his beard as she took his face and held it very close to hers.

"Mama said you were comin', and that I could have a sucker when you did."

"I hope there's a sucker for me too," Ed said, grinning at the girl.

Helen arrived a breath later, just as giggly but grabbing onto his waist instead of jumping at him. "Mama left treats for everyone."

"Well, you girls need some new beds, right?" Ed put Charlene down and glanced behind her to the kitchen and dining room. "Where's your mom and dad?" Maggie usually spent Saturdays in Vernal, but she said she'd be home today.

"In the garden," Helen said, hiding shyly behind Ed's leg.

"You guys remember my friend, Max, right? He's

come to help before. He's gonna put that new bunk bed of yours together."

Max bent down to the girl's height and grinned at them. "Do you guys like gum?"

Ed grinned, knowing that Maggie would likely kill him as he nodded at Max that it was okay to give the girls the treat. Helen came out from behind him and Charlene snatched for the piece of pink bubble gum.

Max held it out of her reach. "First, I need to know. What's your mom making for lunch?"

———

"Hey, beautiful." Ed leaned against his truck, his back still aching at a pain rate of three out of ten. His sister had not only had him and Max move out two twin beds and put together a new bunk bed for the girls, but she'd needed a sleeper sofa moved into the basement too. And that thing didn't come apart and weighed a *lot* more than Max was used to lifting.

But the sight of Jazzy Fuller skipping toward him in a muted navy blouse and a black pencil skirt lifted his spirits. She could barely walk in the skirt, so the skipping was particularly impressive.

She wore a smile the size of Jupiter too, and she giggled as she got within arm's reach. "Hey. No stripes." She paused and scanned him.

Ed felt very much like her eyes were equipped with

lasers, as his skin heated everywhere she let her gaze roam. "I'm glad our schedules finally lined up."

Something flickered in Jazzy's eyes, but it disappeared as fast as it had come. "Sorry, it's been a busy week."

He groaned as he pushed off the vehicle. "I hear you. So." He exhaled and put a smile on his face. He'd been dreaming of going out with Jazzy again, and now that the time was here, he didn't want to discuss his week. He didn't want to talk about the gratitude in his sister's eyes, and the way his nieces had begged him to stay and make cookies with them. He didn't want to mention that Tad hadn't come out of the bedroom, not even to say hello, and that Maggie had made more excuses for him than he deserved.

Jazzy laced her arm through his, and all his cares seemed to evaporate with her simple touch. At that moment, he did want to tell her about all the darker, twisted pieces of his life that he was desperately trying to keep together.

She brushed her hair back from her face, and said, "How do you feel about karaoke?"

Ed scoffed, sure she was kidding. "Oh, I loathe karaoke."

Her face fell slightly, and he realized that she hadn't been kidding. "It's just too loud for tonight," he said, revealing something about himself he hadn't been planning on. "I want...something...quieter." He barely managed to string together the sentence, unsure of how to articulate it to bring back her smile.

She searched his face, understanding appearing in those bright blue eyes. She softened and said, "We can go to China Isle. Most people do take-out, so the restaurant is usually really quiet."

Ed liked Chinese food as much as the next person, so he nodded and turned to open the truck door. Jazzy wiggled her way onto the seat, barely leaving enough room for Ed to position himself behind the wheel.

The China Isle parking lot held plenty of cars, but Jazzy had been right. The majority of the people were waiting in the to-go line. He and Jazzy got a table in the corner at her request, and with the dim lighting and the distance from the entrance, Ed got the quiet atmosphere he wanted.

He grinned at her, relaxing now that they were alone and there was peace in this place. "Thank you," he said. "I...had a stressful day with my sister and...yeah. Thank you."

"How is Maggie?" Jazzy sipped her water before making a face and setting it down. "Okay, that's warm."

A waitress appeared and Jazzy told her about the water. She waved down a busboy, and a fresh water was brought, their order taken, and then they were left alone again.

"Maggie's...overwhelmed." Ed's head ached and he drank half his water in the hope that he was simply dehydrated from all the physical activity of the day. "I do what I can to help her, but sometimes it doesn't feel like enough." He tried to smile, but it felt weak on his face.

Jazzy reached across the table and covered his hand with both of hers. "You probably do more than you think."

"I'm sure that's not true." Ed didn't need to be immortalized or patronized. "But she's the only sibling I have, and I'd do anything for her." His convictions were right there, always first and foremost in his life.

"You moved here to help her, didn't you?" Jazzy asked, her bright blue eyes blazing with knowledge.

"I did."

"Did you—?"

"Can we talk about something else?" Ed finished his water, never more grateful for the speed of Chinese food as the waitress arrived with their dishes. He flashed her a smile, wishing he'd cancelled his date. He wasn't fit to be around people tonight, and he'd known it as soon as he'd left his sister's house.

"Of course we can," Jazzy said without missing a beat. She didn't seem affronted by his brusque tone, and she started chatting about the strawberry festival at the end of the month. Ed had attended a few times since he'd come to Brush Creek, and he let her talk, something she was very good at.

The mood lightened under the power of her voice, and Ed finally snapped out of his funk about the time the cashew chicken disappeared completely. He wanted to apologize, but Jazzy didn't seem to mind carrying the conversation.

He drove her home, unsure of where they stood,

especially when she fell silent. He rarely only took a woman to dinner and then dropped her off, the entire date taking about an hour, but he pulled into her apartment parking lot with a sigh.

"Sorry," he said. "I should've rescheduled." He ducked his head, a pin of guilt pushing into his heart. "I was a lousy date tonight. Can I have a do-over?"

He turned toward her, hoping she housed a lot of forgiving bones in her body. She gazed at him before reaching up to trace her fingers down the side of his face. Tingles shot through his jaw, and his pulse started to pound as she leaned into him, her eyes drifting closed.

The next thing he knew, Ed was kissing Jazzy, and the tingles turned into fireworks. They popped and sparked through his whole system, and Ed brought his hands up to cradle her face.

She giggled and put a breath of space between them. "You want a do-over on this?" she asked, her face still so close Ed could count her eyelashes.

He only answered with another kiss.

CHAPTER 7

"You *kissed* him?" Jazzy's voice could've disturbed a field full of birds, and Fabi did not appreciate it. "He thinks you're me!"

"Oh, relax." Fabi made her voice as carefree as possible, though she'd been fretting over the most delicious kiss of her life since the night before. She and Ed had sat under the huge tree behind the apartment building way past dark, talking and kissing until Fabi was sure she'd never be able to go out with another man without comparing him to Ed.

"Relax?" Jazzy had abandoned her makeup, something she took great care with on the Sabbath. Her eyes were wide and filled with shock. "*Relax?* You realize that word travels very quickly in this small town, right? What happens when someone says they saw me holding hands with Max at the park and then someone says, no, Jazzy's dating Ed Moon?"

"No one concerns themselves with our lives," Fabi said, knowing she wasn't quite right. Whether she liked it or not, as a Fuller, their lives were under more of a microscope than normal. "Most people in this town can't even tell us apart."

Jazzy pursed her lips, and Fabi's brain caught up with her mouth. "And why would people say they saw you holding hands with Max in the park?" She squinted at her twin, who suddenly had an insane amount of interest in her blush brush. "They'd just think it was me."

Jazzy swept the color onto her cheeks, though they filled with a heavy dose of embarrassment. By the time she spoke, she looked positively like a tomato.

"What did you do?" Fabi asked, her chest tightening.

"I told him the truth." Jazzy slammed her precious makeup brushes onto the counter. "Okay? I told him I was Jazzy and you were Fabi, about how you asked me to take your place, all of it."

Fabi didn't realize coldness could be so sharp or seep so quickly through her lungs and into her bones. "When?" She pressed one hand to her heart while her mind whirred through possibilities for damage control. Did Ed already know? Had Max said something to him?

"Thursday night," Jazzy said matter-of-factly. Fabi had never really disliked her sister. They got along great for how much time they spent together, and she couldn't imagine life without Jazzy to come home to, tell everything to, and fall asleep with her in the same room.

But in that moment, she felt a flash of frustration so

strongly she wanted to leave the room and not talk to Jazzy for the rest of the day.

Thursday. She'd told Max on *Thursday* that she wasn't Fabi. And Max and Ed worked together on Friday. But Ed had said nothing on Saturday.

Panic seized her lungs and squeezed. Maybe that was why he'd been in a foul mood at the China Isle. Fabi had thought that was because of his sister, and she'd been happy to sit somewhere quiet with him, eat her favorite crab Rangoons, and wile away a couple of hours giggling, whispering, and kissing.

She looked at herself in the mirror, reassuring herself that he wouldn't have kissed her if he'd known she wasn't who she claimed to be. Would he?

"Do you think he told Ed?" she finally asked. Fabi hated how puny her voice sounded, but she'd never had to hide anything from Jazzy, and her vulnerability leaked into her words.

Jazzy had finished her makeup but she hadn't left the bathroom. "He said he wouldn't, because I told him *you'd* tell him."

Relief rushed through Fabi, though she still had no idea how to tell Ed she was the twin who kissed most of the males she went out with.

And she'd just done it again.

Still, she didn't think Ed would break things off with her now. He seemed...different than the men she normally dated, and Fabi could pinpoint why.

He was real.

He was older than the twenty-somethings she'd been out with recently.

He had more to worry about than what his hair looked like or what he should do now now that he'd finished college.

"How did Max take the news?" Fabi asked. Maybe she could get some pointers on how to reveal her true identity to the man she was rapidly becoming attached to.

"Okay, actually." Jazzy tilted her head the slightest bit. "You really like Ed, don't you?"

"Is it that obvious?"

"Yes."

A smile tugged at Fabi's mouth but she tamed it back into a straight line. "I do like him, and it's a bit strange, but I think this could be something…real with him."

The grin Fabi had smothered appeared on Jazzy's face. "I think so too," she said. "For you and Ed, and me and Max." She giggled, and it had been such a long time that Fabi had heard Jazzy sound so gleeful, that a push of happiness ran through Fabi.

She didn't want to ruin that for her sister. "I'll tell him," she said.

"When?" Jazzy challenged.

Fabi had no idea. "I'm not sure when I'll see him again, so—"

"Today," Jazzy interjected. "Call him and ask him to

meet you for a picnic after church. Or take him up to those waterfalls you like so much. Or ask him to drive to the hieroglyphs with you. But do it today."

Fabi swallowed, sure she couldn't possibly figure out a way to tell Ed who she really was in only a few hours, especially because church sat between now and then. But she couldn't deny Jazzy, so she simply nodded.

Jazzy wore a wary edge in her eye, but she nodded and left Fabi alone in the bathroom. Alone to figure out what to say. Alone to admit to herself that she *needed* to do this to keep Ed in her life—right where she wanted him.

She thought maybe she could put things off a little. Another week. She wouldn't have to see Ed until the weekend if she didn't want to. Of course, she did want to, but she could go another few days, just until she figured out what to say.

But the moment she sat down in church, Wren tapped her on the shoulder and whispered, "So I heard you were holding hands with Max Robinson in the park the other day."

Fabi froze, her thoughts coiling around each other. Once Wren knew, Tate would know, and even though Max hadn't said anything yet, Fabi couldn't ask everyone in town to keep her secret.

She shook her head. "That was Jazzy," she said, because it was. And Max knew it was Jazzy, so as long as everyone else did too....

Her heart leapt. Except for Ed. If word got back to Ed that it was Jazzy holding hands with Max in the park, wouldn't he wonder who he'd been holding hands with? Who he'd been kissing goodnight?

And Ed was a smart guy. If he figured out it wasn't Jazzy, he'd know who it was. She needed to talk to him quickly. Part of her wondered if she should leave church and track him down right now.

Then her mother slid onto the bench and escape was out of the question. "Hey, dear," her mother said. "Your great-grandpa is insisting on grilling today. Two o'clock. I've already got the fire department on stand-by." She chuckled and turned her attention to the front of the chapel as Pastor Peters stood.

Fabi could barely focus on the word the man said, which only fueled her frustration. Church was her escape from the real world, from the things about herself she didn't like. At church, she resolved to be better that week, do more good, become the person she wanted to be.

Sure, maybe she took some steps backward some weeks. Maybe some weeks her steps were stumbling. Maybe some she got in a few baby steps. But as least she was trying.

Halfway through the sermon, she pulled her phone out of her skirt pocket and tilted it to the right, away from her mother. *Family picnic at two?*

She read over the text several times, finally sending it

to Ed. Then she added, *I have something to tell you before we go. Want to pick me up at one-thirty?*

Not able to stand staring at her phone while she waited for him to answer, she stuffed it back in her pocket. Her mom didn't approve of devices out during church anyway. Why Fabi cared, she wasn't sure. She wasn't a child anymore, but some lessons had obviously stuck with her.

Her phone vibrated, but she waited several long seconds before she checked it.

See you at one-thirty.

———

Max finished with Matilda's lawn by nine o'clock on Sunday morning. She rewarded him with a pan of freshly baked cinnamon rolls and a smile in her wrinkled face. "You're a good boy, Max," she said as if he were a dog and not a thirty-five-year-old man.

"Thank you, ma'am," he said, noting that the pan of rolls was still warm. No sense in angering the woman who kept him fed. "I'll get the weeds done and the bushes in the back trimmed, and then I'll get out of your hair." He flashed her a smile and headed for his house. "Be right back."

Through a series of texts, Jazzy had asked him if he went to church. Max hadn't been particularly keen on spending his Sunday's in a white shirt and tie, but he'd been raised going to church. He'd told her as much, and hinted that something had happened in his past that kept him from darkening the chapel doorway.

She'd put the pieces together, and sent him a text late last night. *Your ex-wife?*

Max hadn't answered, and he wasn't even sure why. Jazzy knew about Irina, though Max had never said her name. Jazzy just didn't know all the nitty gritty details. And Max didn't want to provide them, because it meant he had to relive them.

He dug the corner cinnamon roll out of the pan and took an ooey, gooey bite, a moan of pleasure sliding up his throat at the taste of sugar and cinnamon and baked bread. After consuming his breakfast, he washed it down with several chugs of milk right from the jug and went back outside to finish the yard work.

Matilda sat in her rocking chair on the front porch and watched him work. Max hated to admit it, but he could hear Birdy chattering from his place as he clipped rose bushes and trimmed hedges in the back yard.

By the time he finished, the summer sun beat down on the town of Brush Creek. Matilda had gone inside, and Max headed home to shower. After he'd washed away the morning's sweat and dressed in a pair of gym shorts and a T-shirt, he grabbed his guitar, intending to spend the rest of his day with a song on his fingertips. Before he could even pluck one chord, his phone rang from where he'd left it on the kitchen counter. He swiped it on with a smile when he saw Jazzy's name on the screen.

"Hey, beautiful." He opened the fridge to reach for a bottle of water.

"Max," she said, a little on the breathless side.

He abandoned his quest for a drink. "What's wrong?"

"I slipped and fell." Pain radiated through her words. "I'm sorry to call you. My sister just left and...." She panted the words out, and Max swiped his keys off the hook by the door that led to the garage.

"I'm on my way," he said. "Are you bleeding? Did you hit your head?"

She groaned, and Max ran for his truck. He kept talking to Jazzy on his quick drive over, and when he got to her apartment, he knocked loudly but went right in. The way his concern for her drove him wasn't lost on Max, and he realized what was happening. After all, he'd fallen in love before.

The scent of salt hung in the air, and Max glanced around, trying to figure out what was going on. He found Jazzy lying on the couch, the phone pressed to her ear and tears running down her face.

"Hey." He took the phone from her and ended her call with him. "What happened?" She obviously hadn't fallen here. And what was that smell? Really salty, a little bit sweet.

Her breathing was still labored and when she opened her eyes, it took a moment for them to focus on him. "You're here."

"What happened?" he repeated.

"I spilled some marinade in the kitchen," she said. "My grandpa is grilling this afternoon, and my mom wanted me to bring the soy sauce chicken."

"All right." Max took her talking as a good sign, and now he knew that the saltiness in the air belonged to soy sauce.

"I had just put it in the cooler for transport, and Fabi left, and then I realized the bag was leaking all over the place. I stepped around it to get a washcloth, but I stepped in it. It's mostly oil and I went right down." She wiped her eyes, the tears gone now. "I feel like a fool."

Max wiped her hair off her face and smiled gently at her. "No reason for that, sweetheart. People have accidents."

"I did the splits, and let me tell you, I am not that flexible. I think I pulled my groin."

"Is that what hurts the most?" He scanned her from head to toe, his analysis of her long legs and curvy hips purely medical. He brushed her hair back again. "Did you hit your head?"

"I think so, yes. It's my back that hurts the most."

"Can you sit up?" He put his hand on her upper back as she tried to get up and guided her. She sucked in a breath as she straightened fully, and Max said, "Yep, I'm taking you to the hospital."

Her panicked eyes met his. "Really? You think it's that bad?"

"You can't even sit up without pain, sharp pain I'm

guessing, from the way you gasped." He lifted his eyebrows. "Yes?"

"My back." Her eyes filled with tears again, and Max wanted to sweep her into his arms and assure her that everything would be fine. Everything would be fine because he was there, and he was going to take care of her.

But Max knew better than anyone that he couldn't take someone else's pain as his own. That he couldn't make some hurts better. That he couldn't fix everything, even when he tried really hard.

But he could take Jazzy to the hospital and make sure she could use the only back she had for another day.

"If you can't walk, I'll carry you," he whispered, very aware that he was letting out the soft parts of his emotions. He'd vowed he'd never do that again, but something about Jazzy had him unlocking all the padlocks on his heart. Almost like she was the key and he couldn't keep his feelings contained even though he was trying.

Her eyes met his, and that fantastic charge that had always existed between them surged. He saw more in her expression than he'd expected, and he wondered if she'd ever been in love. The way she looked at him, Max certainly felt the glow of affection, and the desire to kiss her reached epic proportions.

Not the right time, he told himself. But at least now he knew—Jazzy wanted to kiss him too.

"All right," he said, sweeping one arm around her

back and slipping the other under her knees. "Hold on, sweetheart. The emergency room is waiting."

She squealed as he lifted her and cradled her against his chest. Then her arms came around his neck, and Max didn't care that he was only carrying her because she couldn't walk herself. It still felt really nice to have this woman in his arms.

CHAPTER 8

Fabi paced in her mother's living room, the cheery sunshine outside the window actually making her nervous. Normally she enjoyed the sun, how it warmed her skin and make her feel carefree. But today it meant Ed would be meeting her family—and he still thought she was Jazzy.

Just the fact that she'd invited him to this barbecue was ridiculous. She hadn't brought a man home in...ever. Never. She'd never brought a man home. That would require dating someone for more than an evening, and Fabi didn't excel in that department.

She'd texted him an hour ago to just meet her at her parents' house, because she was too big of a chicken to talk to him first. But she couldn't say anything to her family either. Number one, her mother would never go along with it. Number two, her brothers would tease her mercilessly if they found out she'd actually been out with someone for several dates and he still didn't know her name.

"You've got to get out of here," she whispered to herself, grasping for any reason to leave this shindig and never come back. It would have to be a good enough reason to satisfy her mother and Ed, who'd seemed excited about the prospect of meeting all the Fullers.

Someone shouted upstairs and then deafening footsteps landed as children ran down from above, one crying and the other yelling.

Ed would change his mind once he got here, and fear struck Fabi right in the chest. What had she been thinking? Ed had one sister—*one*—and two nieces. Fabi was sure they were the quiet kind of nieces, who ate all their vegetables and never quarreled.

Her phone vibrated in her pocket and she practically ripped it out. Ed's smiling face sat on the screen and Fabi almost flung the device into the fireplace. In the end, she answered it just before it was about to go to voicemail.

"Hey," he said. "Have you heard about Fabi?"

"Fabi?" Confusion raced through her, and then understanding hit her like an avalanche. Chills raced down her back. He meant Jazzy.

"Yeah, Fabi. I guess she called Max because she slipped and fell in the kitchen. He's taking her to the hospital."

Fabi seized onto the information and used it like a lifeline. "I'll head over there now." Her mother would likely want to come too, but Fabi could convince her to stay, that she'd go and see what all the fuss was about.

"You don't have to," Ed said.

"Sure I do." Fabi started into the kitchen, where two of her brothers stood talking to their upset children while her mother flurried about, making this salad dressing and then putting cheese on that bread.

"Mom, I have to go," she said.

That got her mother to stop. "Go? Where are you going?"

Even Milt and Patrick cast her a look before sending their kids outside to run off their excess energy.

"Grandpa only grills once a summer," her mom said, laying on the guilt in thick layers. "We never miss it."

"Jazzy's going to miss it too," Fabi said. "She just went to the hospital. I'm going to go see what's going on." She slipped her feet into her sandals.

"The hospital?" The alarm in her mom's voice filled the rafters.

"I'm sure it's nothing," Fabi said. "Ed said she slipped and fell. Max was taking her just as a precaution. I'll go." She practically threw the last two words out of her mouth. "That way, you can stay here and keep everything together." Fabi knew she'd succeeded with that last sentence. She knew what her mother prided herself on, and that was keeping their overly large family happy and content and together.

Her mother finally nodded. "Call when you find out what's going on."

"Of course." With those parting words, Fabi got the heck off her family's property. The last thing she needed was Ed showing up to give her a ride and having to introduce him to someone.

Half a block away from the house, she realized he couldn't go to the hospital either. If he did, he'd see that Jazzy was the one being looked after, not Fabi. She groaned, nothing working out the way she wanted it to.

What should I do? she prayed as she came to the four-way stop at the end of the street.

Of course, she knew what she needed to do: *Tell him the truth.* Why was that so hard? She'd never had a hard time telling a man that she wasn't interested in him, that she didn't want to go out again—or that she did.

She pulled to the side of the road and looked into her blue eyes. "He likes you. It doesn't matter what your name is." But she didn't quite believe herself. No matter what, she had to do something before he found out which twin she was from somewhere or someone else.

With the phone dialing, she found she couldn't breathe very well. The line rang, and every instinct in her told her to hang up and pretend she'd accidentally called him. Then he said, "Hey, Jazzy. I just pulled into the parking garage at the hospital."

"Will you wait for me?" she asked, praying with all her might that he'd say yes.

"Sure. Everything okay?"

"Actually, it's not." Fabi thought she'd wanted to tell

him in person, but suddenly, telling him over the phone sounded like a much better idea.

"Oh. Well. What's going on?"

She drew in a breath and couldn't push the words out. Silence hovered on the line, the tension building until Fabi herself thought she'd snap.

"Jazzy?"

"That's just it," Fabi said, grabbing onto the name that wasn't hers. "I'm not Jazzy."

Now it was Ed's turn to fill the air with nothing. "I'm sorry. What?"

"I'm Fabiana," she said. "There was this mix up and it's really funny actually." She started to laugh and she couldn't rein in the giggles. She sounded one second away from madness, and she felt like it too.

"You're not making any sense," Ed said, his voice taking on a dangerous, dark current Fabi didn't like. "Mix up?"

"I have to go," she blurted. "My mother's calling." She hung up, the guilt over her little white lie plunging deep into her chest. She stared out the windshield, this perfect summer Sabbath surreal and far from her grasp.

What had she just done?

"You blew it with Ed," she said to the glass in front of her. She'd let go of men before. She'd been dumped before. But somehow, this time it was different.

This time it was different, because this time it was Ed Moon who she couldn't have.

"I'M FINE." Jazzy may have enunciated the word *fine* a bit too much. But she couldn't bring herself to care. First Max had waited on her while she was in the hospital. It was only for a few hours, but it felt like weeks. She hadn't torn anything or broken anything. Just a pulled groin and a bruised back. Nothing to do but rest and take painkillers, which she'd been doing for six solid days now.

If she had to spend one more day in the recliner Kyler had brought over, she was going to scream.

Fabi, the target of Jazzy's snarkiness, backed away. "I was just asking," she said.

Jazzy sighed, the apology she should say pooling beneath her tongue. Fabi had worked all their jobs alone this week. She'd brought home dinner, and she'd disappeared into their bedroom when Max came to visit.

She hadn't said anything about Ed, but she hadn't gone out with him either, and Max had whispered a few things to her while he snuggled Jazzy in his arms in the evenings. Something about how Fabi had told Ed who she really was, and now Ed didn't know what to think or what to do.

Jazzy, drugged up at the time, hadn't said anything. But now that her pain was receding and she was getting back to her normal self, she wondered why Ed's and Max's reactions were so different.

"Fabi, I'm sorry," Jazzy called into the kitchen where

her sister worked. "If I go slow, will you walk with me in the park?"

"Tonight?"

"Yes, tonight. I have to get out of here."

Fabi came around the couches and sat on the coffee table, her eyes wide and fearful. "We can't go to the park tonight."

"Why not?"

"It's the summer concert series," Fabi said like that explained everything.

To Jazzy, it did not. When Fabi didn't offer any further explanation, she said, "So?"

"So Ed will be there, working the first aid station."

"So you two did break up."

Fabi's gaze fell to her hands. "I'm not sure we were even dating."

"You were kissing the guy," Jazzy said. "Trust me, he thought you two were dating." Jazzy watched her sister, the deflated posture of her shoulders, the way she sighed like the world was about to end. She'd never seen Fabi act like this after a break up. In fact, Fabi's relationships never really got to "together" status, thus there was nothing to break up.

"Have you called him?" Jazzy asked.

Fabi shook her head.

"Maybe you should."

More shaking, a little more emphatically.

"Why not?"

Fabi finally looked up. "He has my number, and the

ball's in his court." She stood and started toward the kitchen again.

"Oh, come on," Jazzy said. "Since when do you like it when the man is in control of all the balls?"

"Since Ed."

Jazzy opened her mouth to argue and found that she couldn't. If Jazzy had been going through the town directory, she would not have matched her sister with Ed Moon. But seeing them together for the past couple of week, and watching Fabi this past week since she'd told Ed who she really was, Jazzy thought they were perfect for each other.

"I'll call Max and see if he'll walk with me."

"He's doing the adopt-a-dog again."

"Fine. Wren."

"Etta has a summer cold."

Jazzy's blood boiled. She *had* to get out of this apartment. "Fabi," she whined. "Please go with me. I can't stay here for another second."

"I'll call Nana Ebony."

Jazzy would take a trained monkey if it meant she didn't have to stay caged behind walls, listening to her sister sigh every so often and hum to herself that sad, melancholy tune.

Nana Ebony wasn't going to be able to catch Jazzy should she fall, but no one mentioned that as Jazzy navigated the steps to ground level behind her wiry grandmother. "Thanks for coming to get me," she said, giving the older woman a smile.

"Of course. Grandpa isn't feeling well, and it's such a beautiful night." They walked between the antique shop and the bookstore, and the southern edge of Oxbow Park spread out before them. The drum of music in the distance could be heard, and the air was filled with a charge that Jazzy really needed.

The scent of cotton candy and strawberries filled the air as she followed Nana Ebony through the mess of cars in the big parking lot at the end of the park. When they finally reached the footpath, Jazzy had to request to sit down. But she wasn't going back. Oh, no. She'd finally gotten out, and she'd probably have to be dragged back to that apartment.

Plus, she wanted to find Ed and talk to him. Explain. Help. Something.

They finally made it to the big, open, grassy area where the concert was in full swing. Booths had been set up on the north side of the field, and music lovers could enjoy strawberries and cream, churros, cotton candy, and dozens of other foods. Jazzy didn't want anything to eat, though. She only had eyes for the large white tent that said FIRST AID on it.

She sent Nana Ebony in search of a pair of frosted lemonades, and then she walked as quickly as her tired body would take her to the first aid station. Ed's booming laugh filled the air, encouraging Jazzy to limp a little faster.

To her left, the sound of barking dogs almost distracted her, but she kept on toward her goal. She saw a brown-haired man elbow Ed and nod in her direction, and when Ed turned and locked eyes with her, all his joviality disappeared.

Jazzy faltered for half a step and then strengthened her resolve. "Hey," she said, leaning against the folding table. "I'm in dire need of some painkillers."

"Jazzy," he said with a wariness in his voice she didn't understand.

"That's right." She suddenly realized she didn't have anything prepared to say to him. "Look, Fabi's miserable." Oh, her sister would *kill* her for that. "I mean—" She cut off when hope entered Ed's eyes.

"It really was a misunderstanding," Jazzy said. "See, Max asked Fabi out, and she wasn't able to go right away. They'd rescheduled a few times. So when she got the flu on the day of their date, she convinced me to go in her place." A light popped on in her head. "So it's really my fault. I went out with Max, and I kinda liked him too much to give back to Fabi. And he suggested maybe you'd like to double with my sister—which you totally did, by the way. That wasn't a lie. It was just a name thing."

Ed folded his arms. "A name thing."

"She never pretended to be someone she wasn't. I'm the one who did that, and Max...never mind. The only thing wrong was the name." Jazzy wasn't sure what she'd said to cause the edge to enter Ed's eyes, but comparing him to his best friend probably wasn't the wisest course of action.

"She likes you," Jazzy said as Nana Ebony came through the crowd, her hands full of lemonade. "She wants you to call her."

"She knows my number," Ed called after her.

"The ball's in your court," Jazzy tossed back. "At least Fabi thinks it is." She moved away from the first aid station before Nana Ebony could spot her and demand to know what hurt. Truth was, everything hurt.

She accepted a frosted lemonade from her grandmother and drank greedily before saying, "I think I'm ready to head back home."

CHAPTER 9

Max had learned that Jazzy liked simple. She did not want to go to Clive's—that was all Fabi. She did not like mushrooms—again, Fabi. She liked walking in the park and getting day-old bread from the bakery to make French toast for dinner. She liked cuddling into his side and falling asleep. She liked asking him about his family and she'd mentioned several times she'd like to meet Birdy.

Well, today was that day. Max had the weekend off, and he'd invited Jazzy for breakfast at his place. Nerves flowed through him at the thought of her being here, in his house, where Irina had once been.

He had more to tell her about his first wife, and loads more to talk about before they moved to the next phase of their relationship, but in Max's mind, he was ready to take at least a baby step in the serious direction.

And that meant a kiss with the woman who'd been plaguing his dreams for a solid month.

She'd recovered well from her fall, though when he'd discovered she'd walked from her apartment to the park and all around it, he hadn't been happy. She'd only been six days out from her fall, and Fabi had told him she'd slept for thirteen hours that night.

Still, he wasn't her doctor even if he did feel extremely overprotective of her. He'd mentioned that he'd like her to take it easy, and then he'd made sure she did. Another week had gone by, and she'd gone back to work and laid off the pills.

He'd gotten up way too early to start breakfast, as Jazzy wouldn't be coming over until ten. So Max put some birdseed in the cage and took his guitar out to the backyard. He really wished he had a dog to toss a ball to, but he pushed the desire away as he positioned his guitar across his lap.

Maybe there'd be a time in his life where he could get a dog, but it wasn't now. He'd only plucked through a couple of songs before his phone rang.

"Cathy," he said, a note of surprise in his voice. "It's early for you, isn't it?"

"I have a job, remember?"

"Ah, yes. The overnight newspaper. I can't believe there's still somewhere printing newspapers."

She grunted, her usual response to Max and any views she didn't want to discuss further. "So I haven't actually been to bed yet. I did, however, just get off the phone with Mom."

"Oh, boy." Max couldn't help smiling, because he now knew why his sister had called. "And she told you about Jazzy." Max may have mentioned he was seeing a new woman. His mom hadn't made a big deal out of it, though they both knew it was a very big deal.

"Your *girlfriend*." Cathy nearly singsonged the word, as if Max hadn't had a girlfriend before.

He ran one hand up the back of his head. "Not really, Cath. It's not quite official or anything."

"What does that mean?"

"It means...I don't know. We haven't defined anything."

"Are you seeing her today?"

"Yeah." Max wasn't sure why today mattered. He hadn't seen her since Wednesday, when he sensed she'd had enough of him for a while. Jazzy's patience had worn thin easily since her accident, and Max understood why. She was in pain almost all of the time, and she'd never had an experience where she had to rely on someone else quite so completely.

He went through the details of what he was doing that morning, omitting the part where he wanted to kiss Jazzy, and then said, "I still have Birdy. I hope he doesn't terrify Jazzy."

"He's nothing but a softie," Cathy said. "She'll love him."

Max seriously doubted it. In fact, he wasn't sure how

anyone could love the cockatiel, but he kept that to himself. The call ended, and he went back to his guitar, letting his thoughts wander with the notes.

It wasn't until his doorbell rang that he realized he hadn't even started breakfast yet. He jumped to his feet, the guitar making an echoing sound as he moved. He checked his phone, but of course Jazzy was right on time. He'd never known her to be early or late, but always arriving precisely when she was supposed to. This morning was no different.

He hurried through the house and opened the front door to find the gorgeous sight of her face, those pale blue eyes and full lips. She wore a pair of black shorts and a pink sleeveless blouse that enhanced the blush in her cheeks. The fabric looked smooth and soft and Max wanted to touch it.

"It smells decidedly un-maple-like," she said with a flirty smile. "I thought we were eating here?" She glanced past him as if an army of sausages would make themselves known.

"We are," he said. "I just lost track of time."

She nodded to the guitar in his hand. "That was you playing, wasn't it?"

His face heated, and his pulse bounded through his body. He felt too old for such reactions to a woman, and yet he couldn't quiet them. "I guess so." He put the guitar down, embarrassed she'd heard his meandering tunes. "My sister called, and I got distracted. Come in."

He stepped back, hoping the light cleaning he'd done the night before would be good enough.

Jazzy scanned the room, as he knew she would. He had decent furnishings, mostly leftover from Irina's decorative touch. At one point, he'd thought about selling his house, and a realtor had told him to put plants out for a pop of greenery and a hint of freshness. So he had a tall plant in the corner beside the television he never watched. Two on the end tables flanking the couch, which was a dark shade of denim. Irina had spent six months shopping for the cream, blue, and green rug on the floor, and Fabi's gaze stayed on it for longer than the other furniture.

"This is nice," she said, giving him an accepting smile.

Birdy chose that moment to let out an ear-splitting screech.

"Birdy," Max chastised, lunging for the blanket he kept nearby to cover the cockatiel. He tossed it over the cage, but that only sent the bird into a squawk-fest for the ages. Matilda would surely be knocking on his door at any moment. It wouldn't matter, because he couldn't hear anything anyway.

He tried laughing, but it was strained, and Jazzy had backed herself against the front door. Max wanted to drop-kick the bird as far as he could, but he'd settle for just getting it to be quiet. He sent a prayer heavenward that God could somehow silence the fowl so he could enjoy his morning with Jazzy.

Miraculously, Birdy quieted a few moments later, and Max moved into the kitchen to get out the sausage he should've started a half an hour ago. "Better late than never, right?" He glanced over his shoulder and gestured Jazzy closer. "The bird doesn't bite. Well, he actually does, but only if you stick your fingers in the cage."

The tension between them broke, and Jazzy slid her hand up his arm, making him pause. "What can I help you with?" she asked.

"Nothing." His voice sounded like he'd swallowed a cue ball. "I was making you breakfast, remember?"

"And then you forgot." She gave him a playful smile and added, "I can scramble a mean egg."

"How are you with French toast? Because that's what I was going to make."

"Killer." She set about his kitchen as if she belonged there, and Max babysat the sausage as the scent of meat and vanilla mingled in the air.

"So I wanted to talk to you about my ex-wife," he said, his words barely louder than the sizzling sausage.

"Oh?" Jazzy didn't even glance at him, but checked the temperature on the griddle he'd set on the counter for her. She slathered butter on it, which melted into a bubbling froth immediately.

Max summoned all his courage about the same time Jazzy doused a thick slice of bread in the egg mixture she'd made and laid it on the griddle.

"She wanted...our marriage ended because she...." Why was this so hard?

Jazzy finished filling the griddle with French toast and looked at him, her eyes beautiful and wide and accepting.

"She had four miscarriages before she left me," Max said. "I wasn't enough for her, and when I couldn't give her a child, it was over." The words felt like they had knives on the letters, slicing his throat as he spoke.

Jazzy's mouth opened into an O and then she stepped effortlessly into his arms, despite the pair of tongs he held. "I'm sorry, Max." Her voice was as soft as her skin, her curves. "Did you want kids too?"

"Yes." But he'd been satisfied with Irina. She'd been enough for him. Unfortunately, that street hadn't gone both ways.

Time stalled with Jazzy in his arms, the feminine, floral scent of her hair infusing his every breath.

"I want kids too," she finally said, easing away from him one inch at a time.

Max met her eye. "Yeah?"

She lifted one bare shoulder into a shrug. "My mom had nine kids. I think one or two less than that would be ideal."

Max gaped at her for a moment before realizing she was kidding. He laughed, and she joined in. He liked the sound of their combined voices, especially here in his house. It hadn't had a womanly visitor in a long time, and a sense of...rightness hung in the air.

"Families are fun," she said. "But mine's huge, and I

don't think I have even a tenth of the patience my mother does."

He shook the pan, sending the sausage links jostling over each other. "I'm sure you do."

"Remember how I had my sister call my grandmother to break me out of the apartment?" She giggled, a cute little sound that wormed its way right into Max's heart. "I think this is ready. Want me to heat up the syrup?"

He stepped to get it out of the cupboard at the same time she reached for the plate to put the French toast on. His hand collided with her arm, sending the plate into the air. Max caught the plate as it bobbled, and then her wrist as she gasped.

Their eyes met, and Max tugged her closer, thrilled when she came willingly. "I haven't dated anyone seriously since Irina," he said, not sure where the words had come from.

"Haven't hardly dated anyone at all," she said. "If the rumors are to believed."

He cocked his head, trying to hear more behind her words. "You been asking about me around town?"

Jazzy's coy smile sent his heartbeat into a frenzy. "Maybe."

A chuckle rumbled in his chest, but he turned serious a moment later. "How do you feel about maybe you and me becoming more serious?"

"What would that entail, exactly?"

"Oh, you know." He kneaded her closer, bringing his

other arm around her and holding her against his chest. "A little of this." He leaned down and swept his lips along her jaw, every cell in his body flaring to life with the nearness of her, the mere possibility of kissing her.

"Mm," she said. "That's not so bad. What else?"

Max took a moment to flip off the stove so the sausage wouldn't burn. Then he returned to Jazzy, his eyes fastened on her mouth. "A little of that." He dipped his head, moving within an inch of her, letting her either meet his kiss or have the option of stepping away.

He'd never been happier than when her lips touched his. There one moment, gone the next. He growled, the sound part predatory and part desperation, as he sought for a better connection.

Their lips met again, and this time, Jazzy kissed him properly. He kissed her back, creating new memories in this house that had seen so much sadness, making things between them serious, and feeling like this kiss was the beginning of something bigger than anything he'd had before.

CHAPTER 10

By the time Ed felt like talking about Jazzy, or Fabi, or whichever Fuller twin he'd been texting until all hours of the night, holding hands with, and kissing, there was no one around to talk to.

Max had a date with Jazzy, and while his partner had been shooting him furtive glances for the past week, Ed hadn't brought up the topic of the Fuller twins. Max obviously knew who he'd been dating, which only made Ed feel more foolish.

He'd spent more hours in the gym this week than humanly necessary. To combat that, he'd spent more money at the bakery, earning him quizzical looks from Erin, who now wrapped his tarts and piece of peach pie before he even ordered.

Since Max was out, Ed walked down the street and found his sister and her husband sitting on their front porch, hand-in-hand. He paused, the scene narrowing to just the two of them. How they'd survived everything they'd been through was a mystery to him. But they had. And not only that, they seemed to be closer than ever because of it.

Charlene and Helen rode their bikes in the driveway and down the street, calling to each other and then him when they spotted him. Their calls drew Maggie's attention, and she waved him over.

"What brings you by today? I told you I wasn't going to Vernal."

Ed exhaled heavily as he sat on the bottom step in front of her. "Yeah, I know. Just bored, I guess."

"Bored?" Maggie's incredulity wasn't appreciated, but Ed had shown up willingly.

"You're never bored," she said.

"Maybe today he is," Tad said, and Ed was glad, grateful, that his brother-in-law was in a good place today. He could use an ally, and he hadn't been able to go to Max the way he had in the past.

The silence went on a beat too long, which meant Maggie and Tad were communicating nonverbally, something Ed had seen them do in the past. Just not a conversation about him, and he didn't like it.

He waved at Charlene when she called to him to watch her ride with only one hand, and then he said, "So I should probably call her, right?"

"If you like her," Tad said at the same time Maggie said, "Who?"

"I just feel like...." Ed hated talking about how he felt,

and he disliked even more that it was Tad who knew the town gossip and not his sister. He turned toward the pair of them. "How did you find out?"

"I went to Ruby's for breakfast on Tuesday," Tad said matter-of-factly. "Dawn and McDermott were there, and you know how news travels in Brush Creek."

"I don't," Maggie said, her dark eyes flashing.

"Oh, I was dating Jazzy Fuller. But not really. It was really her twin, Fabi." *And I didn't know, and I feel stupid about it.*

Maggie pulled in a breath as her eyes widened. Ed turned away from her so he wouldn't have to see her shock, experience her surprise. He watched his nieces circle each other, their high-pitched voices and childish laughter bringing him the comfort he needed.

"I can't believe they'd do that," Maggie said.

"Well, they did." And by the slightly bitter note in Ed's voice, he still wasn't ready to call Fabi and talk it through. "How do you guys feel about Pieology tonight? My treat."

"I feel great about that," Tad said, as Ed had known he would.

"We don't need pizza," Maggie said, her typical response.

"Great." Ed stood and walked across the lawn. "I'll be back with pizza soon." He was taking a chance going into town. After all, he could run into Fabi anywhere, as he'd learned that she usually had a date most nights of the week. He'd even entertained the idea of her going out with someone else during those long weeks when he hadn't seen her until the weekends. But he'd dismissed the idea quickly.

She may be a flirt and date a lot of men, but she wasn't a cheater. She'd seemed genuinely sorry about the switcheroo, but she sure hadn't stuck around to talk about it much. Ed didn't like that. If there was something he wanted to do, it was get everything out in the open. See what he was playing with. Make decisions with the whole picture.

"Which is why you should call her."

Her sister's words had been hanging in his head for days. *The ball's in your court. At least Fabi thinks it is.*

So he knew she wouldn't be calling him. He wasn't sure why he was so hung up on this woman. He'd been out with her several times, over the course of three weeks. So they'd kissed a few times. It wasn't like they'd talked about their future together, children, or marriage.

Maybe Ed had allowed himself to go too far down the relationship road, and now he was paying the price.

He pushed into the newest pizza joint in town to find a long line. Didn't matter. He had nothing but time. He'd only been standing there, pretending to be completely absorbed in his phone, when he heard a terrifyingly familiar voice.

His head jerked up though he told himself to ignore the woman who'd been plaguing him since he'd met her in that one-bedroom apartment weeks ago. He found her easily, with her gorgeous face and straight, white teeth.

But this wasn't Jazzy.

"Fabi," he told himself, not caring that he was alone on a Saturday night in the Pieology line, surrounded by couples, and now apparently talking to himself. "You went out with Fabi."

The blonde woman he saw every time he closed his eyes, the one with the A-line cut, was holding hands with Max. Not the woman he'd kissed.

Not Jazzy.

Fabi.

Jazzy and Max crowded around a table with a couple of other people Ed couldn't quite see. And he didn't want to see who they were. He didn't want to be there at all. The line went right past their table, and he'd have to talk to them.

His feet itched to turn and go, but his phone chimed, showing him Tad's preference for the shepherd's pie pizza. Made with a mashed potato crust, it really was one of the best pieces of food Ed had ever put in his mouth.

His phone sounded again, and Max lifted his head as if he'd heard it. But in this crowded restaurant, surely he hadn't. They did sit across from one another for hours and hours on end, and Ed would certainly recognize Max's notification noises.

Sure enough, his bus partner scanned the crowd until his eyes landed on Ed. He said something to Jazzy, who whipped her attention down the line too, but only Max came toward him.

"Just getting dinner," Ed said before his friend could say anything. "For me and Mags and her family."

Max nodded and stopped, sticking his hands in his pockets and watching Ed in that annoying, older brother way he had. Jazzy drifted closer, and Ed almost bolted. She looked exactly like Fabi, and though Ed knew intellectually that it wasn't her, he didn't want to talk to her. Surely Max could understand that.

"Just wanted to say hello," Max finally said. "We—I stopped by earlier, but you weren't home." The questions came through loud and clear: *Were you home and ignoring me? If not, where were you?*

"I took the girls out to the bluffs today." And it had been windy and hot, and Ed had to keep a vigilant eye on everything from the weather to the girls to which step he took next. The activity had left no room to think about Fabi, which was why he'd suggested it.

Max nodded, and ducked his head when Jazzy approached and touched his arm. She leaned in close to whisper something to him, and he nodded. Everything happened in slow motion, giving Ed the perfect picture of their easy relationship. He wasn't sure how, but he saw something in those few moments that revealed how much Max and Jazzy got along.

Jazzy met Ed's eye, an apology in hers. Ed took it though he certainly didn't need it, and she left.

"Fabi's on her way," Max said.

"Ah, my cue to leave then." Ed could pick up something else. There were plenty of choices in Brush Creek, and Tad liked a lot of them.

"You don't have to go."

"I'm not talking to her here." He swept his gaze around the restaurant, which was easily filled to capacity. "I'm fine, Max. Really."

His best friend stepped closer, preventing Ed from moving forward in the line. Maybe he could put his order in and wait for it outside, around the corner, out of sight.

"Anyone with two eyes can see you're not fine."

"I went out with her a few times. It wasn't a big deal."

"You're a terrible liar."

"When did you know?" Ed challenged his friend. "Why didn't you feel like an idiot? Like you couldn't show your face to her again?" Better question was, why did Ed feel like that? He'd dated other women, some a lot longer than a few weeks with a few dates on the weekends. But none had given him the charge Fabi had. None had made his heart leap at the simple thought of seeing her. None had invited him to their family's barbecue.

Everything with Fabi had been different, and Ed had allowed himself to get wrapped up in her quickly. Why, he still wasn't sure. But he didn't want to apologize for it. He didn't want to overanalyze it. He just wanted to figure out how to stop feeling like he'd been duped by the town flirt.

And she wasn't even known as the flirty one. *Fun* was what two guys in the office had said. *Non-committal* another had told him. *Flighty. Forward, but not too forward. Likes to laugh. A good cook. A hard worker. Faithful.* Hardly any of the adjectives other guys had given him painted her in a bad light.

In Ed's mind, he'd placed her on a pedestal, and everything she'd done had been perfect.

Instead of answering his questions, Max nodded his ball cap toward the doorway. "She's here."

———

As soon as Fabi spotted Max—which honestly wasn't hard. He was tall, standing a head above most people in Pieology—she froze. He faced her, but he was talking to Ed, who had his back to the door.

Her wonderful, strong, kind Ed.

Her heart gave a little twist in her chest, and Fabi wanted to turn and leave. She didn't need a scene in a public place. And she didn't need to eat another slice of pizza after all the sweets and treats she'd been consuming since making that fateful phone call almost two weeks ago.

Ed spoke with Max for a few seconds, then he turned and came her way. How he could move with so much grace and power was beautiful. He paused a healthy distance from her, making her muscles twitch as though he contained a powerful magnet and some metal shavings had been inserted into her bloodstream.

"Wondering if you'd like to take a walk with me." His

voice was gruff, torn along the edges, but at least he'd spoken. Fabi couldn't even get herself to do that.

She nodded, and he waved for her to go first. Jazzy knew what Fabi liked, and she'd bring something back to the apartment. The evening air still held the heat of the summer's day, and the smell of tomato sauce and roasting meat made Fabi's mouth water.

Pieology sat on the edge of town, where trees grew as tall as giants. Instead of walking back toward town and maybe into Oxbow Park, Ed chose to go west, up toward the canyon. That would become a hike if they went for long, and Fabi was wearing the wrong shoes for such a thing.

"Look," she finally said when it was clear he wasn't going to do any talking. "I'm sorry." With eight brothers and sisters, she'd learned that an apology was always a good way to start a hard conversation. "I never meant to hurt you."

"I know that," he murmured. "And you didn't hurt me."

His words stung, but Fabi wasn't sure why. "All right, then." They made it to the end of the block, the scent of lumber heavy in the air from the expansive yard in front of them.

She paused, sure things could end right here. She could hug him and scamper back to her sister. She'd avoid him for a few weeks and then someone else would ask her out, and—her heart rebelled at the idea of going out with someone else.

In fact, she'd already told someone no, she couldn't go to dinner with them. She didn't want to start again, make the small talk, any of it.

"Why didn't you call?" she asked, deciding on the spot that she wanted to push this conversation, push him.

He sighed, the sound full of frustration—and whether he wanted to admit it or not, hurt. "I felt...I feel...." He didn't finish, but Fabi didn't really need him to.

"Duped," she supplied.

"Betrayed," he said, looking right at her. His eyes were dark, and hard, and Fabi hated the danger she saw in them.

"Like you should've known."

"Like I started to fall for someone I didn't even know." His words flew like straight arrows, piercing her in the softest parts of her chest.

"I started to fall for you too," she managed to say, hoping it would be enough.

It clearly wasn't, because Ed stuffed his hands in his pockets and turned north. This new path would at least keep them on semi-level ground, and Fabi went with him because she didn't want to be left alone in the IFA parking lot.

They circled the block, approaching the red brick church where Fabi would hopefully find some relief the following morning. An idea landed in her mind as if someone else had stuck it there.

"Do you want to come to church with me?" she asked.

Ed's steps slowed, then picked up again. He didn't glance at the red brick building across the street. He edged closer to her, his hand brushing hers on one step and taking hold on the next.

"Can I bring my nieces?"

Surprise shot through her. "Sure. Yeah, of course."

"Can I hold your hand during the sermon?"

Warmth filled her whole body, though they'd left the trees behind and the evening sun was scorching hot. "I don't see why not."

He stopped, squeezed her hand, and looked right into her eyes. His other hand came up and cradled her face. Fabi couldn't help leaning into his touch, a sigh passing her lips as her eyes drifted closed.

"Maybe can we start over?" Ed asked. "Maybe we can go on back to Pieology and have our first date there."

Fabi's eyes shot open, and she easily got lost in the dazzling depths of his dark eyes. "Yes, let's start over. I'm Fabiana Fuller. I'm five minutes younger than my twin, Jazzy, who's still a bit peeved with me that she has short hair." A smile flitted across her face. "She hates short hair."

Ed tucked one of Fabi's long ends behind her ear, the touch simple yet sensual at the same time. "I like yours."

Fabi, who had kissed men on the first date many times before, lifted up on her toes and said, "I like you," only a moment before kissing Ed.

CHAPTER 11

J azzy enjoyed a week of normalcy. No worries that someone might call her the wrong name in front of the wrong person. No drama over a fall. No pain, either, thankfully. No more watching Fabi drift around the apartment aimlessly, starting one task only to leave it unfinished.

They worked through their homes with the precision and efficiency they'd long ago perfected. They met up with Max and Ed in the evenings. Fabi claimed to have started over with Ed, but Fabi saw them kissing under the trees behind the apartment complex. Of course, maybe that was Fabi starting over.

They didn't double again, and as another week went by and July marched toward August, Jazzy started to toy with the idea of inviting Max to the weekly Fuller family dinner.

She entered Ruby's one Tuesday afternoon to meet

him for lunch, determined not to go to her next job without inviting him. Fabi hadn't seen what the big deal was, but Jazzy knew it was something. Just because Ed sat beside her every week in church now didn't mean Fabi thought that was unimportant or had somehow trivialized it. She knew people had seen them. She knew bringing a man to church was a declaration of something serious.

Jazzy knew too, which was why she hadn't done any of those things. She scanned the crowd at Ruby's and didn't see Max. They'd gone a little slower, spent more time talking than anything else. She sensed he still had a few things to tell her about his ex-wife, but he hadn't brought her up since their breakfast weeks ago.

Jazzy suspected he still wasn't over Irina. The whole house screamed of her, from the plants to the rug to the fact that Max hadn't let anything go except the woman herself. In fact, Max had a very hard time letting anything go, as testified of by the cockatiel he hated but kept for his sister.

Her mouth pinched into a tight line at the thought of the bird. She really didn't like it, from the way he made such a ruckus, to the heaps of birdseed strewn all over the floor. The maid in her had wanted to tidy up before eating, but she'd refrained.

She wanted to go back to Max's often, because that kiss in his kitchen had opened a door to a new life. One Jazzy wanted to experience daily, with Max at her side.

The bells on the door jangled, and she turned to find

him there, a wide smile on his face. "Hey, beautiful." He wrapped her in a hug that made her feel loved and accepted. Max had a special way of looking only at her, even in a crowd, and it was something Jazzy was still getting used to after so many years of being passed over.

"Sorry I'm late. Did you order already?"

"I've literally been standing here." Thinking. Too much thinking. Jazzy needed to get out of her head—something Fabi was forever telling her—and just let herself live.

"Well, let's go sit. I only have forty-five minutes."

"Busy day."

"Meeting with the shift supervisor." He flashed her an easy grin and followed the hostess to a booth against a wall of windows.

He'd barely sat when he said, "So I have something I've been wanting to ask you." His blue eyes bounced around the diner now, seemingly unable to settle on hers.

Jazzy's heart did cartwheels inside her chest. "All right."

"I was thinking maybe it's time to take you home," he said. A blush filled his face instantly. "Wow, that came out wrong. I've been tellin' my family about you for weeks, and I'm wondering how you feel about going to Vernal with me to meet them."

Jazzy reached across the table and covered his hands with hers. "I was going to invite you to the Fuller family dinner tomorrow night." She grinned. "So yeah, I think it's about that time."

Max swallowed, the hesitation right there on his face. "The Fuller family dinner?"

"Every Wednesday, at my parent's house. People come if they can. It's casual."

"Will everyone be there?"

"Probably not. The only time everyone is together in one place is when my mom mandates it. The family dinner is more relaxed than that."

"Sounds great."

"I'll let her know we're coming." Jazzy caught Max's panicked look and added, "Just so she knows how much food to prepare." Not like that really mattered. Her mother cooked for an army no matter how many people were coming. She didn't know how to make a meal for only two, which was why Jazzy's parents went out to eat most evenings.

"So what about this weekend? Want to go to Vernal then?"

"Sure." Jazzy felt like someone had encased her internal organs in gelatin. Why was she all wobbly at the thought of meeting Max's family?

Because it's a big step, she answered herself silently. A step she'd never actually taken before.

Max tapped on his phone and sent a message before looking at her again, his eyes dazzling when they danced like they were now. "Great. It's all set."

"Great."

———

THE NEXT EVENING, Jazzy didn't feel so great. She knew she looked great—Fabi had told her a hundred times. Her hair had started to grow out, and she'd had Starlee even it out so it was less A-line and more chin-length bob all around.

She wore a pale blue sundress which Fabi claimed made her look like a golden goddess. But Jazzy didn't think goddesses dealt with as much anxiety as she currently was. She slipped her feet into a pair of white ballet flats and went downstairs. Her mother hummed as she plucked grapes from their vines, and she smiled as Jazzy sat at the bar opposite her.

"You look miserable," her mom said.

"I'm...fine."

"Is Max not coming?"

"He's coming." It was everyone else Jazzy wished weren't coming. But tonight, of all nights, she'd learned that everyone in her family would be at the dinner. The only people missing would be Brennan and Cora, and only because they lived in California.

But Dawn and McDermott would be there, with his little girl, Taya. McDermott often brought his Nana Reba too, and sure enough, she was coming tonight. Patrick and his family were coming, as were Milt and his entire crew. Kyler and Dahlia, who'd been back in town for a few weeks now, had confirmed that afternoon. Wren and Tate never missed the weekly dinner, and Wren said it was because she needed a night of good food she didn't have to make herself.

Fabi was coming, albeit alone. Her sister hadn't brought Ed to the family dinner yet, but the cuddling at church had definitely reached epic proportions. Even Berlin, who rarely came to any family functions anymore, had emerged from the woodwork to say she'd be there that evening.

Her mother still had her pinned with a meaningful look, so Jazzy said, "I'll go get Grandpa," mostly to get out of the conversation. She took her mother's minivan and went around picking up all the older generation of Fullers. Three more pairs of eyes to scan Max and deem him worthy or unworthy.

She came down the road to find half a dozen cars parked in the circle driveway in front of her parent's place. Ignoring the twitch of nerves in her stomach, she pulled into the garage and helped her great-grandfather out of the van and up the steps into the house. A wall of noise hit them, and Jazzy panicked that perhaps Max had arrived while she'd been gone. She hadn't seen his truck or his motorcycle out front, but she still scanned the group for his handsome face.

Her mother blocked her view, her eyes round and worried. "Your phone's gone off several times." She extended it toward her. "Sorry, baby."

"Sorry," Jazzy repeated as her mom moved away. She wasn't sure why her mother had to be sorry, but she instinctively took the phone and slipped back into the garage to find out.

Max had texted several times and called once. There was no voicemail, but the texts explained everything.

"He's not coming." Her voice echoed in the garage, though it housed four cars. She reread the messages. "He's not coming because of that blasted bird." She let her hand fall to her lap, a keen sense of disappointment and disbelief coursing through her in a dangerous cocktail.

After all, she'd lost many dates to Fabi over the years. Even a few to other women, to a sport that took a man out of state.

But she'd never lost to a cockatiel before, and it felt like a new low in this new life she suddenly didn't want.

————

FABI HUDDLED close to Ed on the park bench, as if two other people were sharing the seat made for three. Truth was, she just liked being close to him. Their do-over had been going extremely well, and Fabi was sure the past few weeks of her life had been a fantasy. A dream. Something she made up to convince herself that she could get up and get through one more day.

And then she'd see Ed, and his whole face would light up and she'd remember that this life wasn't fake.

"What did she say?" he asked, his voice little more than a whisper.

"She didn't say anything." Fabi fiddled with his fingers, her worry over her sister somewhat new for her.

"But Max didn't come to the family dinner tonight, and he was supposed to."

"That doesn't sound like Max."

"Right? That's what I told Jazzy, but she just disappeared upstairs. When she came down, she'd changed out of her new dress and she snuck out the back right as dinner was served." Fabi hated that she didn't know where her sister was, that she hadn't answered any of her calls.

Ed said, "Maybe she just needs some time to be alone."

"We're never alone," Fabi said. She stared across the path and past the fence that separated them from the lake. "I just don't like not knowing."

"She's a big girl," Ed said, not unkindly. "She's probably at home, waiting for you right now."

Fabi settled further into Ed's chest, a sigh leaking from her body. "You think so?"

"Maybe," he said.

But when they crossed the street and ducked down the alley to the apartment building, Fabi didn't see a light in their second-story apartment window. "She's not home." She marched around the front of the building and up the steps, Ed right behind her.

Sure enough, the apartment sat dark and empty. It felt stale, like no one had been there in days, though both Jazzy and Fabi had left it only hours earlier. She spun back toward Ed. "It's late. Where is she?"

"It's barely ten o'clock, love." He brought her close,

held her against his heart. He'd started calling her love last week, and it made Fabi feel loved. She enjoyed the sense of safety and peace coming from inside the circle of his arms, and she almost relaxed. Almost.

"I have to go," he whispered, nosing her neck in a way that sent tingles down her arms. "I'll call you first thing in the morning, okay?"

She nodded, too distracted to kiss him goodnight. She closed and locked the apartment door and settled onto the couch to wait.

Fabi woke with a shooting pain in her lower back and a wicked kink in her neck. Sunlight streamed through the kitchen window behind her. The apartment was still, silent, eerie.

"Jazzy?" she called though she knew her twin wasn't there. Hadn't come home. She checked the bedroom anyway, only to find two made beds, one of which Marbles was curled up on, purring.

Desperation and helplessness like she'd never experienced rushed through Fabi. She fumbled to find her phone, finally locating it in the front pocket of her purse, where she always kept it.

She tried Wren first. "Have you heard from Jazzy yet this morning?" The twins had a job they needed to start within the hour to stay on schedule for the day.

"Nope." Wren didn't seem to know that Jazzy, the stable, predictable, albeit giggly, sister had dropped off the face of the earth. "So you've got—"

"She didn't come home," Fabi blurted. "She left dinner early last night, and I don't know where she is."

"Oh." Wren squeaked. Or maybe that was her toddler.

"I'm going to call Dawn. Maybe she's seen her." Fabi hung up without waiting for Wren to answer. Dawn had gone through some hard times of her own over the past few years, and while she'd removed herself from the family, Jazzy had never let Dawn get too far away. Fabi had secretly envied Jazzy for the way she always seemed to know exactly how her siblings were doing, and she realized it was because Jazzy wasn't self-centered.

Dawn's phone rang and rang, finally being picked up by McDermott, who said, "Hey, Fabi. Dawn's still in bed."

"Oh, of course." She worked late at night, cleaning the businesses the family had contracts with. "I was just wondering if either of you have seen Jazzy."

"Just at dinner last night." He didn't seem concerned, and Fabi wasn't sure she wanted to get the police involved. But she'd now called Wren—whose husband was a police officer—and McDermott, a state trooper.

"Okay," she said, making her voice falsely bright. "Thanks, McDermott."

"Do you want me to have Dawn call you when she gets up?"

"No, it's fine." Fabi let her hand drop to her side, her mind reeling. She thumbed out a quick text to Wren, asking her to reschedule their jobs for the day. Jazzy was more important than dusting or vacuuming.

Then she turned in a slow circle, taking in the apartment she'd shared with her sister for seven years. They'd wanted to move out of their parents' house together, but neither wanted the responsibility of a mortgage. When this apartment building went under construction, they'd come to look at the floor plans, and they'd put down a deposit before the place was even finished.

Fabi loved her quaint little apartment, and she couldn't imagine living here without Jazzy. She seemed to see her whole life in front of her, and she knew intellectually that if things progressed down the same path she was already on with Ed, she wouldn't live in this apartment forever, period.

He owned a home on the east side of town, near his sister and the wilds of Utah. Fabi supposed if they got married, she'd move in with him, leaving Jazzy the apartment to care for herself.

"Not gonna happen," Fabi said with great conviction. Because she was going to find her sister and figure out what had happened with Max. And then they were going to fix it. Because Max and Jazzy belonged together, even if they couldn't see it yet.

She grabbed her purse and marched toward the door, her phone out again. This time, she called her sister, the prayer that she'd answer fierce and flowing freely from her lips as she left the apartment.

CHAPTER 12

Jazzy ignored her phone, just like she'd been doing for the past twelve hours. She caught the flash of Fabi's name on the screen, and a pinch of guilt traveled down her spine. But her sister could wait.

"You sure about this?" Starlee held the bottle of hair dye, her hands already gloved, her eyes full of doubt.

"Completely sure."

"Maybe you should just talk to Fabi first."

"Fabi doesn't get to decide what color my hair is." Not anymore. Not again. Jazzy was tired of being passed over in favor of her sister, or a job, or a stupid bird. A *bird*. Not that becoming a brunette would change that, but her hair color was something she could control, and those items were in limited supply at the moment.

"Maybe you should take a night to sleep on it."

"I slept on it." Jazzy had done very little sleeping, but

Starlee could probably tell that just from the bags under Jazzy's eyes.

The stylist drew in a deep breath. "All right." She applied the toner to Jazzy's hair, the coolness of it meeting her scalp and sending a wave of relaxation through her tense muscles. All Fabi had to do was get online and look at Jazzy's bank account to figure out where she'd stayed last night. There was only one hotel in Beaverton, but it had been far enough outside of Brush Creek City limits to satisfy Jazzy.

Max had called twice, and Jazzy had sudden clarity as to why Ed hadn't wanted to speak to Fabi. She may have blamed him for a day or two, but she saw now that his reasons for taking a break were valid.

That was all she needed. A break. Some time to figure out what she really wanted with her life. All she knew right now was that she wasn't continuing it as a blonde.

———

MAX GLARED at his phone like it was the reason Jazzy hadn't called him back. He'd been at his desk for ten minutes, and he hadn't moved a muscle. Hadn't fired up his computer. Hadn't opened a file. He just needed to talk to her.

Ed entered, and he cast Max a look that reminded Max of a kicked dog. "What?" he practically barked.

"Fabi's worried about Jazzy," he said, his voice

completely level. "I guess she didn't come home last night."

Max's heart dove for the floor, burrowing through his other organs, causing them to twist painfully. "She didn't?" He stood but Ed gave him a stern shake of his head.

"She's looking for her now."

"I'll call her."

"I bet you've done that already." Ed shifted piles around his desk like he was really organizing it. Max had seen this diversion many times, and he knew that Ed didn't organize anything. The man's house looked like a bomb went off on a daily basis. His dogs didn't help, as they liked to chew stuffed animals until the stuffing was strewn all over the place.

Max sat down, looking as helpless as Ed had ever seen him. "Leave it for now," he said.

"But what if she's hurt?"

Ed gave his best friend a pointed look. "Of course she's hurt."

Confusion pulled at Max's brows, ran rampant through his system. "What does that mean?"

"It means you chose to stay home and take care of your sister's bird over coming to meet your girlfriend's family." Ed spoke slowly, in his calm paramedic voice, and though Max had done that, he didn't realize he had done *that*.

"She's my girlfriend," he said, the words not quite lining up in the right order. Or maybe they were in the right order. Maybe he'd just never put them together quite that way.

"Of course she is. You've been dating her for almost two months. You're kissing her and all of that. What would you call that?" Ed jiggled his mouse and the black screen of his computer brightened. As if he was going to do any work right now. He hadn't even taken a sip of his coffee yet.

"Birdy was freaking out." Max realized how lame his excuse was. But he hadn't wanted to leave the fowl as he didn't want to disturb Matilda, who hadn't been feeling well. His intentions were good. Weren't they?

"I have to talk to Jazzy," he said.

"Give her some time," Ed said. "I know she probably needs it."

"But she should know—"

"And you've got to do something about that bird," he continued as if Max hadn't said anything at all. "And probably your whole house."

"My whole house?"

Ed removed his hand from his mouse and looked at Max. "What have you thrown away since Irina moved out?"

Max opened his mouth, a whole stream of words parading through his mind. None of them came out.

"Exactly," Ed said. "I'll come over on Saturday. We'll purge. Then you can call Jazzy."

"She'll call me before then," Max said, his voice full of confidence he didn't feel.

Ed grunted, and that ended their conversation. By lunchtime, Max found himself praying for a multi-car accident he could run off to. At least then he would feel useful.

Nothing came in. Not even the silly schnauzer who liked to climb on top of the barn. Max made it home and glanced next door to Matilda's place. He couldn't hear Birdy, though a dog barked somewhere down the street. The air was still, deathly almost, and Max went past his front door in favor of Matilda's, his paramedic radar pinging in his head.

He knocked and called, "Matilda? You home?" Her car was in the driveway, not an inch out of its usual place. Somehow, something was wrong. "Matilda?" He tried the door and found it open, as usual.

Her little lap dog, a puffy white Bichon Frise that Matilda had had as long as he'd known her, streaked past him, a couple of yaps coming from its mouth. The dog bounded down the steps and relieved itself on the lawn while Max turned his attention back to the house.

It smelled like the whole place needed to be aired out, and he left the front door open as he entered. A plate holding a single piece of toast sat on the dining room table, the only oddity in the house.

He called dispatch and asked if anyone had been sent to her address. Nope. But Matilda wasn't here, and she should've been. She hadn't been feeling well.

"You must be Max."

He spun at the masculine voice, his muscles tensing

to fight or run. A tall man stood in the living room dressed in business attire, the tie around his neck seeming to throttle him.

"I am." Max glanced at the little dog who'd followed the man inside without so much as a warning yip. "Who are you?"

"I'm Charlie," he said, extending his hand. "My mother speaks about you often."

"Charlie." Max smiled and shook the man's hand. "Matilda talks about you all the time too." He glanced at the cold toast. "Where is she?"

"She called last night and said she wasn't feeling well."

"Yeah, she mentioned it to me too."

Charlie nodded and loosened his tie. "When she mentioned chest pains, I got in the car and drove here from Salt Lake. I took her to the hospital about midmorning. They're keeping her overnight for monitoring." He sank onto the couch, making it look like a child-sized piece of furniture. "I hate hospitals."

Max had had plenty of his own experiences inside of hospitals. "I hear you."

"Aren't you a paramedic?"

"Yes. The hospital is usually a beacon of relief. But I've...I've seen plenty outside the scope of my job." He didn't need to give Charlie the details of Irina's fertility issues. The pain he'd endured mentally and emotionally while she dealt with all of that, plus a physical aspect of their loss.

"Well, I'll leave you to relax." Max stepped toward the door. "Sorry to barge in. I was concerned."

"It's fine. I'm glad my mother has a neighbor looking after her." Charlie gave him a tired smile, and Max went home. He wished he had one of Ed's dogs to greet him. Instead, all he had was that messy bird.

He stood just inside the doorway, the birdcage on his right, the rest of his house spreading out before him. Every item he looked at brought a memory of his first wife. When she'd bought the rug. Where she'd picked out the couches. Why they'd painted the mantle a smoky shade of gray instead of black, the way he'd wanted to.

As he stood there, he realized that Jazzy would never be comfortable in this house his ex-wife had built. How he'd lived here for five years with the constant reminders was a sudden mystery to him.

"You haven't been living." His voice whispered through the house, lifted toward the ceiling, full of truth and power. He hadn't realized it, but he honestly hadn't been truly living. He got up. He ate breakfast. He went to work. He saved people. Came home and fed the bird. Mowed Matilda's lawn on weekends.

Repeat. Repeat. Repeat.

He didn't want to simply repeat the same day anymore, especially this one without Jazzy in it.

Desperate and afraid, he dialed her again. It had been almost twenty-four hours since he'd texted and then called to say he couldn't come to her family dinner. She didn't answer, and Max slumped into the dining room chair closest to him.

Birdy yelped at him for more bird seed, or more water, or just because he felt like making a fuss.

Max ignored him and instead decided to cancel dinner with his family on Saturday night. He wasn't feeling confident anymore that he and Jazzy would be in a place to go together. With that done, he faced the house again.

He didn't even know where to start the purging. At least he could see that it now needed to be done. Glancing at Birdy, who clung to his cage with his clawed feet, Max said, "Starting with you."

He reached for his phone and called Cathy. "Look," he said in his nicest big-brother voice. "I have to get rid of Birdy. What would you like me to do with him?"

CHAPTER 13

Ed eyed the pile of boxes and furniture on Max's front porch as he eased his truck to a stop. So his friend had already started the purge. Ed supposed that was easier than trying to convince the man that he'd held onto everything from his past and that he now needed to let it go.

Max exited his house, a rolled-up rug over his shoulder. He took it past the other items and on over to his own truck. The rug was probably the last thing the truck could hold, and he dusted his hands off and waved to Ed.

Ed got out of his vehicle and looked from Max to the truck. "What's left inside?"

"Not much," the other man admitted. He came closer to Ed. "Why didn't you tell me sooner?"

"Tell you what sooner?"

"That I was stuck in the past."

Ed shrugged. "You didn't seem to mind so much.

Not my business. I don't know." He pulled on a pair of gloves. "So point me in the right direction. Boxes in my truck? Where are they going?"

Max gave him directions for the stuff on the porch—all of it was going to the Salvation Army in Vernal. Ed loaded up everything and then stepped inside the house. It hadn't undergone a massive transformation, but just having all the decorations cleared out made it feel sterile, nondescript.

A drop cloth covered the kitchen table, and half a dozen cans of paint sat on top of it. "You're painting?" he asked when Max joined him inside.

"Just the walls and the mantle," he said.

"Where's Birdy?" Ed didn't see him in the corner, nor could he hear the normally rowdy animal.

"I listed him on the Brush Creek Classifieds last night, and we sold him to the Coopers."

"Jennifer Cooper?" Ed's eyebrows went up. "You realize she has three other birds already."

"So what's one more?"

"Cathy agreed to this?"

"Talked to her last night."

Ed saw the new formations for the couches, that the TV had been moved to the opposite of the room. "So I take it Jazzy hasn't called."

Max's mouth tightened and his bright blue eyes flamed with dangerous fire. "No."

"Did you call her again?"

"Yes."

"I told you not to."

"I couldn't help it," he said. "I wanted her to know I'd gotten rid of Birdy." When his best friend looked at him again, Ed found the desperation in his expression. "How do I get her back if she won't talk to me?"

"Time," Ed said. "She needs time."

"Time for what?"

"I don't know. I just know I needed some...time to wrap my head about things."

Max nodded, but he didn't look happy about the prospect of just waiting things out. Sometimes, though, time really was needed to get thoughts aligned and to set hurt feelings aside.

"So you and Fabi seem all right now."

"Yeah," Ed said. "I think we are."

"Serious?"

"Serious enough. I haven't met her family yet. But I don't think we'll break up anytime soon."

"You sit by her family at church, I've heard."

"Just Jazzy."

"Surely her parents have seen you."

"A quick glance is different than a formal meeting. Talking. Answering questions." Ed shrugged. "You'd know more about it than I would."

"Yeah?" Max nodded toward a stack on the counter. "That's trash. You haven't met a woman's family?"

"I haven't dated anyone seriously enough for that in years. Since moving here." Ed picked up a stack of newspapers. "Colorado State University?" He quirked an eyebrow at Max. "What are these?"

"Cathy sends them to me every week. She works at the printer there."

"And you kept them?" Ed knew Max loved his family. He just wasn't sure he'd keep his sister's college newspapers. It wasn't like she'd written any of the articles in them. Of course, Ed had moved across the state to take care of his sister, so who was he to talk?

"I'm throwing them away now," he said. "Purging."

Ed saw a pile of sheets and blankets in the hallway. "What's all this?"

"More stuff that needs to go in your truck."

Ed grabbed the corner of a comforter. "You're getting rid of your bedding? What are you going to use?"

"I'm going to go to the store and pick something out myself." He cast the comforter a look that held a lot of memories behind it and turned away. He cleared his throat and put together another box. "I don't think there's a single thing in this house I picked out. Might be easier to sell the place and move."

"Nah." Ed folded the blanket and reached for a sheet. "This is what you need to do. Go through the past and discard what you don't need anymore." He met his friend's eyes. "Trust me on this, Max. You'll come out the other side happier if you do the work to get there."

"How would you know?" Max challenged. "You've never been married. Gone through anything like what I've been through."

A pinch started in Ed's chest. "You're right," he said. "But I've seen my sister and her husband do the work, and when I see them, I see strong people who know who they are and what they want."

"I know who I am and what I want," Max said in a quiet voice.

"Jazzy?"

Max nodded once and looked away.

"All right then." Ed finished with the linens. "Let's get this place cleaned out and spruced up, and then we'll figure out how to get her back."

———

"I AM SO MAD AT YOU!" Fabi put her hands on her hips and glared at Jazzy as she came into the apartment. Her sister stood in the kitchen, wearing a floral apron over a pair of jeans and a blue short-sleeved sweater that Jazzy had bought her for their birthday last year.

"Where have you been, huh?" Fabi's eyes flashed as she came around the counter. "I've been worried to death. I can't eat. I can't work. Maggie Wainwright has taken our clients for the past two days. No one has seen you or talked to you—what did you do to your hair?"

Jazzy closed the door behind her and entered the living room, carefully placing her purse on the coffee table before she collapsed onto the couch. It felt good to be home, even with Fabi ranting at her. The place smelled like disinfectant, as Fabi was a stress cleaner.

Their apartment was probably the freshest it had been since they moved in years ago.

"I stayed in Beaverton," Jazzy said.

"Doing what?"

Jazzy wished her sister's voice wasn't quite so shrill. "Doing nothing." And it had been wonderful. No computer. No stress. No work. Only her own thoughts and her own desires.

"Why didn't you call me? Or answer any of my texts and calls? I've been worried *sick*!"

"I needed a vacation."

"Fine." Fabi sat at the end of the couch, her knees turned toward Jazzy. "Then we look at our calendars, and we talk to Wren, and we book tickets. We don't just disappear from the family dinner and ignore our family for three solid days."

Jazzy nodded, the tears she'd kept dormant for seventy-two hours finally pricking the back of her eyes. "I know. I'm sorry." Her voice broke, and Fabi was there, gathering her close and stroking her hair.

"He's been by twice," Fabi said. "You should see his face. He's broken."

Part of Jazzy was glad about that. "He made a choice."

"I like your hair this color." Fabi fingered the ends of Jazzy's hair.

"Did you talk to Starlee?"

"You know, I think she's the one person in town I didn't try." Fabi pulled back and looked at Jazzy. She had tears in her own eyes, which touched Jazzy's heartstrings and made her emotional again.

"He chose a bird over me." Her voice came out strangled. "I'm used to men choosing you over me. But a bird?" She scoffed. "I must be really...something. Repulsive. Something."

"You are not repulsive."

Jazzy managed a weak smile. It had taken her twenty minutes to get herself out of her car and inside the apartment. She'd known Fabi would react this way, but she couldn't afford to pay for a hotel room in a town down the road for much longer.

"Do you want to go lie down?" Fabi asked, sweeping her fingers across Jazzy's forehead. In a life where Jazzy had spent so much time taking care of her younger sister, it sure felt nice to have the roles reversed.

"I have chicken in the slow cooker," Fabi continued. "I was about to put rice on, and if you go lay down for an hour or so, dinner will be ready."

Jazzy cracked a smile. "Look who's the responsible one now."

"Oh, don't go giving me labels." Fabi stood. "Ed was going to come over, but I'll call him and let him know you're back."

"I don't want you to cancel with him because of me." Jazzy stood and followed her sister into the kitchen.

"Whatever. It's fine." Fabi fixed Jazzy with a stern look, but her voice wavered a tiny bit when she said, "You're more important, Jazz."

Emotions swelled inside Jazzy again, and she ducked her head and retreated to the bedroom. She didn't feel more important. Stuffed near the end of a long line of kids, Jazzy had stayed out of trouble for most of her life. She'd always had Fabi's shadow to exist in, and she'd always had Fabi to take care of. She and Fabi had talked so much about what they wanted, and now that Jazzy had been presented with the possibility of a life with someone as wonderful as Max Robinson, she'd seized onto it with both fists.

A mistake, she told herself. *Falling for a man who doesn't even realize he hasn't let go of anything in a decade.*

One thing Jazzy had learned over the three days she'd been hiding out in Beaverton was that she had indeed fallen in love with Max. She wasn't sure when, or for how long, but the only way she could describe the depth of her feelings was with the word love.

She sat on the end of her bed, not sure what to do next. She was only tired mentally, and physical sleep did blessedly turn her mind off. She laid back on the bed, a slip of pain trailing down her spine from her fall several weeks ago.

Jazzy ignored it and let her eyes drift closed. She was aware of small sounds beyond the closed bedroom door, but they faded into the background. Jazzy felt like she was floating up, up, and away, and her limbs felt light and airy.

In her fantasy, Max threw a ball to a magnificent

golden retriever, who bounded after it with joy on his face. There were no squawking birds in the background, and no feminine touches in the house where he led the dog to get a drink.

Jazzy hovered above it all, watching the beautiful man she loved from afar, wishing he would look around and see her there. See her at all.

Chapter 14

"I don't know about this." Max shifted his feet as he and Ed stood outside the twins' apartment. "She hasn't called me back."

"She only showed up an hour ago." Ed lifted his fist to knock, but Max grabbed it.

"Maybe I should just go home. Give her the time you talked about."

"Look, man. We spent the day clearing your life of everything holding you back. Are you ready to move forward or what?"

"I am." Max swallowed. "I think." Honestly, he hadn't known until Thursday that he was solidly stuck in the past. Could he really be ready to take a step forward after only one day? He and Ed were just crossing back into Brush Creek when Fabi's call came through, and Ed had put her on speaker.

She's home.

Those words had been moving through Max's mind since Fabi's call. He didn't want this apartment to be Jazzy's home. He wanted to build a home with her, a new life together, but he wasn't even sure he owned all the tools for such construction.

"I'm going to go," he said. "I'm not ready for this." He turned away amidst Ed's protests, but Max knew how he felt. He may not go to Sunday services every week, but he knew how to pay attention to his gut, and showing up only an hour after Jazzy had returned to town—without a phone call—wasn't right.

He gained the bottom of the steps at the same time he heard Fabi say, "Hey, Eddie," in a the fun, flirty tone that only the Fuller girls could achieve.

Eddie. Max scoffed. He'd literally never heard someone call Ed Eddie before. He went outside, knowing Jazzy was inside that apartment but unable to face her quite yet. She needed to come to him, and if she needed time to do that, so be it.

Max went home and changed into an old pair of gym shorts and a ratty T-shirt from his days in the paramedic academy. Then he changed that light gray mantle to the black he'd wanted eight years ago. He made the stark white walls that Irina had insisted would make the smaller space bigger and brighter a shade of robin's egg blue that the saleswoman at the paint store had assured him was the in-color right now.

He painted long after the sun went down, finally collapsing into bed well after midnight, glad he'd physically exhausted himself so he didn't have to spend the long minutes before he fell asleep obsessing over the fact that Jazzy still hadn't called him.

———

THE NEXT MORNING, his phone woke him. A beam of sunlight slanted across his face, blinding him as he opened his eyes and tried to find his phone. A groan tore through his throat and he missed the call.

He fell back to the pillows, the scent of the new bedding still a bit strange in his nose, but he was awake now. Gradually, his eyes adjusted to the light, and a headache made itself manifest. After swallowing some painkillers, he got in the shower, knowing he'd have to re-bathe after he went next door and took care of Matilda's yard.

She'd come home on Friday morning, and her son had gone home Friday afternoon. Max had checked in with her twice yesterday, and he'd promised to get her yard work done today, as usual.

His phone was ringing as he wrapped a towel around himself, but he didn't even try to get it. If it was a job-related emergency, they could call someone else. If it was Ed, he could wait until Max had shaved and eaten. Anyone else...well, his mother or sister could wait too.

He went through the actions of eating and shaving, each movement methodical and managed. When he finally felt like himself again, he looked around the bedroom he'd shared with his first wife.

Nothing of her remained. Not the curtains. Not the bedding. Not the lamp that Max had thought looked more like a piece of art than something he just needed to use to light his way at night.

He and Ed had cleaned it all out, and Max had picked up the essentials at a department store in Vernal. He could go to Preston's here in town and get new curtains and a new lamp and anything he needed. For now, the minimalist way of life suited him just fine.

The house seemed unusually quiet after all the noisy chatter from Birdy. Max didn't miss the bird though, and yes, he knew the Coopers had a few birds already. Birdy would fit right in there, and another flash of gratitude that Cathy had agreed so quickly to get rid of the bird pulled through him.

He picked up his phone, almost ready to go next door to mow and trim.

"Jazzy." Her name wheezed through his lips. She'd called twice.

He pressed too hard against the screen in his haste to call her back, but his doorbell rang before the call even started ringing. He hung up as he went down the hall, needing peace and quiet and time to talk to Jazzy when there wasn't someone at the door.

And who would be stopping by on a Sunday morning anyway?

He pulled open the door, maybe a little too harshly, maybe with a little too much frustration.

A woman with dark hair stood there, glorious and radiant in a white dress printed with brightly colored flowers. Her long legs ended in a pair of bright red heels, and when Max's eyes met hers, he realized it was Jazzy.

He breathed her name again, hardly daring to believe the striking brunette was his Jazzy.

"I'm sorry," she said, lifting her chin a fraction of an inch the way she did whenever she had something hard to say. "I was hoping you'd consider coming to church with me today and then taking a walk through the park."

"No," he said. "No, no, no." He didn't need an apology, not from her. He swept her into his arms and took a deep breath of her skin. That same floral fragrance that followed him into his dreams filled his entire soul.

"No?" she repeated.

He wasn't even sure what the question was anymore. "Don't apologize," he said instead, slipping his lips along her temple, encouraged when she leaned into his touch. He moved his mouth down the side of her face and tasted the soft spot on her neck that made her arch further into him.

"I'm the one who's sorry." He put a couple of inches between them so he could look into her eyes. The desire to kiss her was so strong, so strong, it pulled at him with the force of gravity. "Want to come see what I've done?"

He backed up farther, needing the space so he could make things right between them before he kissed her. He led her into the house, glad when she came with him. She secured her fingers in his as she glanced around.

"No bird," she said. "You've painted. The rug's gone." She scanned the rest of the space before settling her gaze on his. "What happened?"

"All of that stuff was Irina's," he said. "Her rug. Her choice on the colors. The realtor's suggestion for the plants. I...guess I realized that I've been living in someone else's house for five years." He looked at Jazzy. "I got rid of anything I didn't pick myself."

"There's hardly anything left."

"Yep." He didn't like admitting that, but he needed to. "I...my wife took care of a lot in our marriage. She paid the bills. She kept the house clean. She made dinner most nights."

"Mm hm. Did she work?"

"Yes, part time as a teller in the bank." Max liked the silence in the house now that the bird was gone. "She had a good eye for décor, so though we didn't always agree, I just let her do what she wanted. After she couldn't...after we lost the last baby, she decided she needed a change of scenery. I let her do whatever she wanted, no questions asked. She left six months later."

"I'm sorry," Jazzy said again, and Max really wished she'd stop saying those two words.

"I haven't changed a thing," he said. "It was time. I'm ready—" He drew in a deep breath. "I'm ready to start over again."

Jazzy stepped in front of him, dropping his hand to lift hers to his face. "Yeah?"

"Yeah." He leaned his forehead against hers. "I was thinking it would be real nice to start it with you." He put one tentative hand on her hip, not drawing her closer quite yet.

"Hm."

He opened his eyes and looked into hers. "What do you think about that?"

"I think that sounds great."

Happiness burst through Max's chest, chasing away the lingering melancholy over the memories he'd held onto for too long. "Yeah?"

"Yeah."

"I'm sorry about Wednesday," he said. "I have a good explanation if you need it."

"I don't really need it." She glanced over her shoulder to where the bird cage used to stand. "You got rid of the bird?"

"I hated that bird, and so did you. He was part of the purge."

She dropped her eyes, a vulnerability in her that Max wanted to seize and erase at the same time. "You chose a bird over me."

"Matilda next door wasn't feeling well. Birdy was freaking out. I didn't want to disturb her, and so I thought it best to stay home. I'm sorry, Jazzy." He cradled her face in both hands, hoping she could feel his level of remorse. "I'm so sorry. I would never choose a bird over you. You know that, right?"

Jazzy's beautiful eyes looked into his for several long seconds. She finally gave a small nod. "Yeah, I know that."

Max smiled, relieved that she was so good, so forgiving. "So can I kiss you now?"

"Only if you'll get dressed and come to church with me. I'm tired of sitting there by myself."

He'd go to the moon to be with her, so he nodded and said, "If you can find a tie in my closet, I'll go."

A glint entered her eyes and she stepped away from him and down the hall, her heels clicking against the laminate wood flooring he'd actually chosen and which Irina hadn't had the funds to replace before her flight from his life.

Jazzy returned a few minutes later, the ugliest tie he'd ever seen in her hand. "It's the only one you have, but I found one." She looped it around his neck and drew him closer, closer, closer.

"I'm in love with you," he whispered when their lips were merely breaths apart.

She froze, and Max wondered if he should've saved those words for another time.

A smile made her whole face light up. "I love you, too." She kissed him then, a slow, sultry kiss that spoke of her love for him. Max matched it the best way he knew how, hoping she felt cherished and treasured—the way he felt about her.

The Following Christmas

Fabi stood in front of the full-length mirror on the back of the bedroom door, a familiar place for her. She didn't even acknowledge Jazzy's eye roll as she passed her to go into the bathroom.

"Still just as skinny," her twin mumbled before closing the door and turning on the shower. So mornings weren't Jazzy's strong suit. But organizing a wedding certainly was. And not just a wedding, but a double wedding, as she and Fabi were getting married on the same day.

Four days from now.

"The dress fitting is in forty-five minutes," she called.

"I know," Jazzy's muffled voice came through the door. Of course she did. Jazzy had a binder for each of them, with checklists, pricing pages, and sketches of everything from the dresses, to their faux fur shawls, to the lighting at the reception.

None of her siblings had gotten married in the winter, and there were certain challenges for guests, the venue, and the brides-to-be with four feet of snow on the ground. All the other married Fuller family members had gotten married outside, except for the emergency move into the firehouse that Brennan and Cora had been forced to do.

But Jazzy and Fabi had opted to get married in the chapel where they'd grown up listening to sermons. Pastor Peters would have the honor of making them wives, and Jazzy had taken care of everything. The date. The booking of the venue. The decorations. She was organized almost to a fault and Fabi had let her do her.

Fabi, on the other hand, had played to her strengths too, and that included consulting on what they should have. She came up with the ideas, or approved them, and Jazzy executed them.

For a moment, a blip of a sadness crossed her features. In four days, this apartment where she and Jazzy had lived for seven years would be empty. Dawn said she'd clean it while the twins were on their respective honeymoons—Fabi had excelled at vacation planning since she was a teen, and she'd booked a trip for her and Ed to the beautiful big island of Hawaii.

Jazzy had wanted to go somewhere a little more quaint, and she and Max were going to Banff for a few days of skiing, sight-seeing, and snuggling near the slopes.

An hour later, she rushed Jazzy through the doors of the dress shop in Maple Mountain. "We're late."

"It's fine," Jazzy said, the frustration in her voice. "This place isn't even open yet."

"Exactly," Fabi said. "Georgie came in early just to meet us."

"You were the one who couldn't stop gazing at yourself in the mirror."

"I was not."

A tall, dark-haired beauty came out of the back room, a long, white gown in each hand. "Hello, ladies."

"Georgie!" Fabi squealed and hurried forward as fast as she could in the heels she'd worn. She needed them in the insanely long dress she'd chosen to get married in. "Oh, Jazzy, look at them."

Georgie hung the dresses on a tall rod, letting the trains fall down. Fabi ran her fingers along the buttons that ran along the shoulders of her dress, admiring the lace on the bodice, and the masterful way the dress had been altered to ensure the neckline wouldn't reveal too much cleavage.

"Tina is waiting in the back for you, Jazzy," Georgie said with a wide smile. "Fabi, you're with me."

More squeals came from Fabi's throat. She couldn't help it. Jazzy took her dress and went down the hall, and Georgie picked up Fabi's and told her to follow. She went in the dressing room with Fabi and helped her with the dress, pulling it over her hips and adjusting it across her shoulders.

"It's perfect, Fabi." She zipped it up and stood back, looking at Fabi in the mirror.

Fabi ran her hands down her body, the feel of the wedding dress against her skin almost too much for her to process. "I can't believe I'm getting married," she whispered. And to the love of her life. Fabi had never felt so lucky and grateful at the same time, and tears filled her eyes.

"Get the tears out now," Georgie said. "You don't want to be weepy on your wedding day when you've got all that makeup on." She beamed at Fabi and gave her a hug from behind. "Just a few more days, right?"

Fabi nodded, too emotional to speak.

———

IF SHE THOUGHT she was emotional when she tried on her dress, it was nothing to the storm of happiness, joy, sadness, anxiety, and the general attitude of freaking out that happened on the morning of her wedding.

Fabi made it through the curling of her hair, which she'd grown out. The makeup, which Patrick's wife did. The dressing, which her mom and Nana Ebony had helped with.

Now she stood in the bride's room with Jazzy and everyone else had gone to take their places in the front row of the chapel.

"I can't believe this," Jazzy said. "I always knew you'd get married before me. I just didn't think it would only be by a few minutes." Jazzy gave her a hug, and Fabi closed her eyes, wanting to commit this moment to memory.

"I can't believe we're not going to live together after this."

"Kyler said he and McDermott would move everything while we're gone."

Fabi straightened and smoothed down her dress. "I know. It will be good, I know. I'm just sad."

"We'll still work together every day," Jazzy said. She ran her hands down her dress too, which was simpler than Fabi's, without as much lace, but with stunning pearlescent beading on the bodice.

Jen, the wedding planner Jazzy had been working with, poked her head into the room. "We're ready for you, Fabi." She gestured for Fabi to come forward. "Jazzy, I'm going to send you with Alonzo. He'll take you up to the balcony so you can watch but no one will see you yet." She grinned and Fabi gave Jazzy one more hug before following Jen to the foyer.

Her father waited there, and Fabi beamed at him. "Hey, Daddy."

"You ready, peanut?"

"So ready."

"Ed's at the end of the aisle," Jen said. "Remember to walk slowly. Your photographer can only get the pictures you give him. Flowers here." She handed Fabi a bouquet of exquisite flowers in shades of blue, pink, and cream. "Hold them right at your hips, like we practiced."

Jazzy had insisted on a rehearsal for everything, right

down to the dinner that followed the wedding and how to walk down the aisle.

Jen touched her ear and said, "Cue the organist." A moment later, the wedding march began, and she nodded toward Fabi and her father. "You're a go."

For a moment, Fabi felt like her wedding was a covert operation. Then the doors opened and she saw the chapel filled to capacity, all the guests standing, wearing their best clothes, as they watched her walk down the aisle, her forearms pressing right against her hipbones, as instructed.

Her eyes landed on Ed, and all the nerves that had been accumulating since he'd asked her to marry him in September died away. Pure love filled her heart, and she saw it on her future husband's face.

Her father passed Fabi to Ed with a kiss to the temple and a murmured, "She's all yours, son," before he sat beside her mother on the end of the first row.

Fabi couldn't look away from Ed, from his meticulously groomed beard to his dazzling, dark eyes. "Hey."

"Hey, yourself." He swept a kiss along her cheek and they faced the pastor as a pair.

———

JAZZY LISTENED to Pastor Peters talk about love and family and solving arguments before letting them fester into problems. He told Fabi and Ed to communicate with each other, and make goals as a couple, and involve God in their lives.

His speech was beautiful, and then he started the vows. Within a few minutes, Fabi's bright, beautiful, beaming face turned toward Ed and they were pronounced man and wife. He bent her backward while she whooped in surprise and kissed her with a chuckle coming out of his mouth.

He obviously hadn't gotten the memo that their great-grandfather was in the room and he didn't approve of over-the-top displays of affection. The rest of the crowd didn't seem to mind, Jazzy included, and they laughed and clapped.

"Look up here," she whispered as Fabi and Ed started down the aisle, hand-in-hand. They'd trade places for her wedding, which was set to start in five minutes, but she and Fabi had agreed to look up on the way out of the chapel.

Fabi did, and her eyes met Jazzy's. She gave her a double thumbs-up and Fabi laughed just before she disappeared under the edge of the balcony.

Jazzy barely had time to turn before Alonzo said, "We need to go, Miss Fuller." He gestured wildly from the back of the chapel. "Mister Robinson will be coming in any moment, and we don't want him to see you."

Jazzy wanted to see him, though. See him before the doors opened and every eye was on her and she had to look at him with all those people watching.

So she took a couple of steps toward Alonzo, but she

kept her eyes on the front of the chapel, where the altar was.

"Miss Fuller," Alonzo said, his voice pleading now. Jen would probably kill him if he allowed Max to see Jazzy before the ceremony. Jazzy didn't want all that bad luck either, but she really wanted a peek of Max in his tuxedo.

He appeared, his back straight and his shoulders broad as he walked down the aisle, his parents in flanking positions behind him. She'd met them only a week after they'd made up, and she liked his family a lot. He'd come to the Fuller family dinner almost every week since their engagement—something that had happened an hour before Fabi's.

He looked powerful and perfect, and he stopped in his place and pulled on the sleeves of his jacket as if they were too short. His mother adjusted one of his lapels and threaded a pale pink rose through the flower hole.

Jazzy hurried up the last few steps and through the door before Max could feel the weight of her gaze on him and looked up to the balcony. She really didn't need all that bad luck.

She went carefully down the steps to the lobby, the memory of the first time she'd descended steps to go out with Max. She'd pretended to be Fabi then, but she didn't have to pretend anymore.

"Hey, pumpkin." Her father gazed down at her with such love, Jazzy couldn't help leaning into his embrace.

"I can't believe this," she said. "I never thought I'd get married."

"You didn't?"

Jazzy had never said that aloud to anyone, not even Fabi. She shrugged. "Hard to get married when you never date."

"I always knew," her dad said.

"Yeah?" Jazzy searched his face. "How?"

"You have a big heart, Jazmin. You always have. Max is very lucky to have you."

Tears welled in Jazzy's eyes. "Thanks, Daddy."

"Now, let's get you down that aisle."

The doors were opened from the inside, and Jazzy only had two seconds to wonder who had opened it before her father was moving her down the aisle. She forgot the practice session she'd forced Fabi to endure, and took a few steps with her hands in the wrong place and her steps too fast.

Then she heard the clicking of the camera and reminded herself that the wedding photographer she'd hired had not come cheap. She wanted excellent pictures of this day, so she slowed her step and settled her arms into the right spot.

Max's gaze bored into hers, and while he'd assured her over and over that he wanted to do the big wedding again, she still hadn't believed him. Until that moment.

He watched her with the keen interest in his gaze, and his bright blue eyes devoured her from head to toe in her wedding gown. His smile widened and his eyes closed in bliss as he received her into his arms.

"I love you," he breathed into her hair, which she had kept dark and grown back out to the middle of her back.

"You're supposed to wait for that until after the I do's." She giggled, hearing her sister's voice in her head to stop the giggling. But she couldn't. She was a giggler.

"Am I?" He shrugged. "I'm going to say it every day, Jazzy."

Jazzy wasn't sure if she'd ever experienced true joy before, but in that moment. That one, single moment with Max's loving eyes looking into hers, and the sexy smell of his cologne hanging in the air between them, Jazzy was sure the perfection running through her was indeed joy.

"I love you too," she whispered just as Pastor Peters started his speech. It didn't matter what he said—other than the declaration that she and Max were now legally and lawfully wedded—because the most important words had already been spoken.

I love you.

With the ceremony over, she hurried down the aisle, almost forgetting to glance up to the balcony, where Fabi and Ed stood at the railing, smiling and clapping. She lifted her and Max's joined hands, and Fabi whooped while Ed cupped his hands around his mouth and yelled his congratulations.

She and Max spilled out of the church and into the waiting limousine. They were laughing and Jazzy tried to catch her breath as Jen piled her train into the car and then tapped on the roof of the car.

As the limo moved out of the way so the next one could get into position, Jazzy took a deep breath and looked at Max. "Well, we did it."

"Yes, we did." He leaned down and captured her mouth with his, kissing her so completely, Jazzy wondered how she'd ever go a day without this man by her side. Thankfully, she didn't have to.

"I love you," he said again, and Jazzy snuggled into his chest, ready to continue building this new life with Max at her side.

———

Want to read more Brush Creek Cowboys Romance?
Read on for a sneak peek at the last book in this series,
THE CHIEF'S CATCH.

Berlin Fuller looked at herself in the mirror, Starlee standing behind her. The stylist kept running her hands through Berlin's dark blonde hair, waiting for her to give her directions.

"What are we doing today?" shouldn't be such a hard question. Especially because Caitlyn and Scotty were loitering only a few feet away, also waiting.

Berlin switched her gaze to Caitlyn's. A preschool teacher who'd taken the day off for Berlin's transformation, she lifted her eyebrows as if to say, *Go on already.*

Scotty checked her phone, smiling at the screen.

"I want a new look," Berlin said, her voice strong and probably too loud for the nearly empty salon. "Darker hair. Shorter. Make me look...different."

Berlin was tired of her current life, and she was only twenty-seven-years-old. She'd taken as many online courses in accounting that she could, finally finishing her degree a couple of years ago by leaving Brush Creek for Colorado Springs.

She'd dated a couple of guys there, but nothing had stuck. That was how she felt about every man she went out with. Like she was some sort of Teflon and they wouldn't stick around no matter what.

"Darker?" Starlee asked, still combing her fingers through Berlin's locks. "Y'know, most women want to go lighter, not darker."

"Not too short," Caitlyn said, stepping closer. "Still brushing her shoulders. But nothing she can put in a ponytail." She met Berlin's gaze with a meaningful look in her eye. "We're not doing ponytails anymore, remember?"

Starlee looked between the friends. "Is this a hair change or a life change?"

"Life," Berlin said, squaring her shoulders. She'd just had another birthday and it was so exhausting to attend the Fuller family dinners as a singleton. Sometimes she brought Caitlyn along, but now she had a boyfriend. Scotty worked up at the horse farm at the top of the canyon, and she didn't make it down during the week that often.

She put her phone in her back pocket and stepped forward to join the conversation. "We're taking her to the summer fair tonight." Scotty leaned over Berlin's shoulder, her smile wide and beautiful. She wouldn't have any trouble getting a date tonight, not after she curled her miles of dark hair and put on her rodeo makeup. The woman was a former barrel racer, and she had a new man on her arm every weekend. She claimed to like the revolving door of male attention, but Berlin had tired of it quickly.

And at this point, she just wanted a date at all. If she had to go into the empty office for another weekend in a row so she wouldn't have to stay home alone, she might paint the whole thing bright pink. And boy, would that make Wren mad....

"She's not leavin' until she has a date." Scotty giggled. "So darker. Spruced up. Berlin's doing everything different now."

Berlin's doing everything different.

The words echoed through her head. She had told her friends that, maybe in a moment of weakness. Starlee met her eyes and said, "So darker?"

Berlin nodded, her pulse skipping just a little inside her veins.

"What color are you thinking?"

"Something like Scotty's," Berlin said. "Do you think that would work?"

"I just got a new ashy black. Want to try that?"

Ashy black sounded dangerous, deadly, different.

Berlin swallowed and nodded again. She wasn't sure how easy it was to undo something like ashy black, but she suspected it wouldn't be easy.

"I'll go mix up." Starlee left before Berlin could change her mind.

And you don't want to change your mind anyway, she

reminded herself as her friends retreated to find magazines and settle in while the first leg of the transformation began.

———

HOURS LATER, with the new do, ten times more makeup than Berlin normally wore, and with the blouse Scotty had found at the only department store in town falling off her right shoulder, she slipped her feet into a pair of ankle boots.

The jean skirt was a little too tight, and Berlin wouldn't wear it in front of her mother. But her mother wouldn't be at the summer fair tonight. Heck, Berlin shouldn't even be going. Friday night at the fair was usually filled with hormonal teenagers, all looking for someone to sneak away in the dark with.

Berlin's stomach swooped. She didn't want a summer fling. She wanted to meet an interesting man, and the summer fair was the perfect place to show up with her new look.

"So we get to choose," Caitlyn said as if she hadn't reminded Berlin of their bet at least a dozen times since they'd met for breakfast that morning. She had the whole plan laid out, from the salon appointment to the fake eyelashes to the amount of time they could spend shopping.

"I know." Berlin tugged on the hem of her skirt.

"We get an hour to find an appropriate man."

Caitlyn folded her list and tucked it in her pocket. "And whoever we choose, you have to get to ask you out. That's the deal."

"All the boys are comin' down from the horse farm tonight." Scotty looked up from her phone, her smile so wide and infectious Berlin felt herself relaxing.

"I don't like cowboys," she said.

Scotty scoffed as if the idea of not liking cowboys was utterly ridiculous. "They're not all married."

Berlin pressed her lips together, the soft pink gloss Caitlyn had insisted on a bit sticky. It would do no good to argue with Scotty. Berlin had agreed to the terms of their deal, and all she could hope for was that Caitlyn would find someone more concerned about people than he was about his mare.

"All right. Let's go." Caitlyn tucked Berlin's hair behind her ear and then flipped it out again. "You look great."

Her hair was indeed an ashy black which reflected the light strangely in different situations. She liked it a lot more out in direct sunlight, but the fair would be full of fluorescent lights in shades of orange. She shuddered just thinking about what color her hair would be then.

But she couldn't stop the inevitable, and she reminded herself—again—that she wanted to do everything backward than what she normally did. After all, her previous attempts at dating had her going on a double date with a man whose last name she'd never learned, and then a forty-year-old detective who her family had disapproved of because of the fifteen-year age difference.

She'd really liked Gray, but in the end, they were just too different. On two different ends of the life spectrum. And his fourteen-year-old daughter had been a real problem.

"Remember, no one with kids," she told her friends.

"That might be hard," Caitlyn said though she'd readily agreed to it before. "And it won't matter if they're...what?" She peered at Berlin as she drove toward the park. "Under ten?"

"Under eight," Berlin said. One of her sisters had married a widower with a seven-year-old daughter, and Dawn had been brilliant at the insta-mom thing. Berlin wasn't sure she could take on a child at only age twenty-seven, and she certainly hadn't clicked with Gray's daughter. Last she'd heard, he'd started dating an older woman with a couple of teenagers herself. A pang of loneliness hit her, and she pushed Gray out of her mind.

"No cops," she told her friends as Caitlyn found a parking spot and swung the car into it.

"Oh, no," Caitlyn said. "That wasn't part of the deal. You just said no men with teenagers."

Berlin opened her mouth to argue, but Scotty squealed in a volume that could burst eardrums and launched herself out of the backseat. A couple of cowboys loitered by the fence that ran along the walking path in the park, and she threw herself at one of them. He caught her around the waist and twirled her.

The carefree nature of the exchange had Berlin swallowing back a sour jealousy she wished she could never feel again. And yet, she asked, "Who's that?" anyway.

"Him? That's Branch. Her brother. He's been in Montana for years. She said he was going to try to make it."

"Branch isn't a name," Berlin grumbled. "That's another one. Only men with real names."

Caitlyn tipped her head back and laughed. "I have no control over that."

"You know everyone in this town."

"Please. That would be *you*." Caitlyn hipped Berlin, who stumbled sideways for a step as they approached the two cowboys. Scotty made the introductions and everyone started walking toward the festivities on the other side of the lake.

Bright lights lifted into the dark night, staining the sky with light pollution, and the din of noise could be heard from hundreds of yards away.

"An hour," Caitlyn said, skipping ahead and linking her arm through Scotty's. "C'mon, girl. We have work to do before we find guys of our own."

Berlin watched them giggle and hurry ahead, leaving her with Branch and his buddy, Henry. "Drinks are on me, boys."

They were at least smart cowboys, because neither of them argued with her. Scotty had said she'd provide a way that no one else would hit on Berlin until they'd picked out her man, and apparently that came in the form of two cowboys flanking her.

She bought sodas for them and flavored lemonade for herself, and together they camped out on the edge of the fair. The scent of hot oil filled the air, along with laughter and the dinging of bells as boyfriends won stuffed animals for their girls.

Only twenty-four minutes later—Berlin may have put a timer on her phone—Caitlyn and Scotty came pushing through the crowd.

"Got 'im." Caitlyn drew in a big breath, her chest heaving. Whether from excitement or because she needed to spend a bit more time on the treadmill, Berlin wasn't sure.

Her stomach coiled and recoiled, getting ready to strike like an angry snake. She took one more gulp of the sour lemonade and said, "Okay. I can do this."

Scotty gripped her shoulders with both hands and looked right into Berlin's eyes. "You *can* do this. Different. Dark." She giggled again and glanced at Caitlyn. "You're going to *love* him."

"I just have to get him to ask me out," Berlin said. No one had said anything about falling in love, though Berlin yearned to do that. Have someone to hold hands with, whisper secrets to, fall into a kiss with the way her sisters did.

She drew in a deep breath and said, "Point him out."

Caitlyn and Scotty turned back to the crowd, slipping to Berlin's side and pushing the cowboys out. "He's not a cowboy," Caitlyn said. "So don't let the hat fool you." She pointed toward the milk bottles. "There he is. Black hat."

Berlin scanned the crowd, but there were literally a dozen black hatted men near the milk bottles. Her heart pitted and patted and hopped around like a frog on caffeine.

"Police uniform," Scotty added. "Oh, he just laughed."

Berlin's heart sank all the way to her cute little boots. "The Chief of Police?" She turned toward Caitlyn. "You want me to get Cole Fairbanks to ask me out?"

"He's perfect for you," Caitlyn purred, giving her a little shove.

Berlin's jaw tightened and she gave a tight little shake of her head. "He doesn't date," she said. "I'm never going to get him to ask me out." As if she even wanted to. Cole had come to town two years ago when Chief Rasband retired. He was devilishly handsome, sure. A double hit to the heart with that uniform and that cowboy hat, definitely.

And Berlin would not be the first female to try to charm the man since he'd come to town. As she watched a bubbly blonde named Tiffany approach and flirt with the man, she realized she wouldn't even be the first woman to attempt to get his attention *tonight*.

"Go on," Caitlyn hissed and gave her another push.

Berlin was going to fail miserably, but a deal was a deal.

Help me, she prayed with every step toward the carnival games. *Give me the right words. Make him like brunettes with ashy black hair. Just get me through this deal.*

After all, if she lost, her friends had dreamed up a terrible consequence for her, and she would not give them the satisfaction of setting her up on a dozen blind dates.

———

THE CHIEF'S CATCH features the youngest—and last!—Fuller Family member to find true love. I hope you enjoy this Beauty and the Beast retelling. **It's available now!**

The Marine's Marriage: A Fuller Family Novel - Brush Creek Cowboys Romance (Book 1): Tate Benson can't believe he's come to Nowhere, Utah, to fix up a house that hasn't been inhabited in years. But he has. Because he's retired from the Marines and looking to start a life as a police officer in small-town Brush Creek. Wren Fuller has her hands full most days running her family's company. When Tate calls and demands a maid for that morning, she decides to have the calls forwarded to her cell and go help him out. She didn't know he was moving in next door, and she's completely unprepared for his handsomeness, his kind heart, and his wounded soul. **Can Tate and Wren weather a relationship when they're also next-door neighbors?**

The Firefighter's Fiancé: A Fuller Family Novel - Brush Creek Cowboys Romance (Book 2): Cora Wesley comes to Brush Creek, hoping to get some in-the-wild firefighting training as she prepares to put in her application to be a hotshot. When she meets Brennan Fuller, the spark between them is hot and

instant. As they get to know each other, her deadline is constantly looming over them, and Brennan starts to wonder if he can break ranks in the family business. He's okay mowing lawns and hanging out with his brothers, but he dreams of being able to go to college and become a landscape architect, but he's just not sure it can be done. **Will Cora and Brennan be able to endure their trials to find true love?**

The Trooper's Treasure: A Fuller Family Novel - Brush Creek Cowboys Romance (Book 3): Dawn Fuller has made some mistakes in her life, and she's not proud of the way McDermott Boyd found her off the road one day last year. She's spent a hard year wrestling with her choices and trying to fix them, glad for McDermott's acceptance and friendship. He lost his wife years ago, done his best with his daughter, and now he's ready to move on. **Can McDermott help Dawn find a way past her former mistakes and down a path that leads to love, family, and happiness?**

The Detective's Date: A Fuller Family Novel - Brush Creek Cowboys Romance (Book 4): Dahlia Reid is one of the best detectives Brush Creek and the surrounding towns has ever had. She's given up on the idea of marriage—and pleasing her mother—and has dedicated herself fully to her job. Which is great, since

one of the most perplexing cases of her career has come to town. Kyler Fuller thinks he's finally ready to move past the woman who ghosted him years ago. He's cut his hair, and he's ready to start dating. Too bad every woman he's been out with is about as interesting as a lamppost— until Dahlia. He finds her beautiful, her quick wit a breath of fresh air, and her intelligence sexy. **Can Kyler and Dahlia use their faith to find a way through the obstacles threatening to keep them apart?**

The Paramedic's Partner: A Fuller Family Novel - Brush Creek Cowboys Romance (Book 5): Jazzy Fuller has always been overshadowed by her prettier, more popular twin, Fabiana. Fabi meets paramedic Max Robinson at the park and sets a date with him only to come down with the flu. So she convinces Jazzy to cut her hair and take her place on the date. And the spark between Jazzy and Max is hot and instant...if only he knew she wasn't her sister, Fabi.

Max drives the ambulance for the town of Brush Creek with is partner Ed Moon, and neither of them have been all that lucky in love. Until Max suggests to who he thinks is Fabi that they should double with Ed and Jazzy. They do, and Fabi is smitten with the steady, strong Ed Moon. **As each twin falls further and further in love with their respective paramedic, it becomes obvious they'll need to come clean about the switcheroo sooner rather than later...or risk losing their hearts.**

The Chief's Catch: A Fuller Family Novel - Brush Creek Cowboys Romance (Book 6): Berlin Fuller has struck out with the dating scene in Brush Creek more times than she cares to admit. When she makes a deal with her friends that they can choose the next man she goes out with, she didn't dream they'd pick surly Cole Fairbanks, the new Chief of Police.

His friends call him the Beast and challenge him to complete ten dates that summer or give up his bonus check. When Berlin approaches him, stuttering about the deal with her friends and claiming they don't actually have to go out, he's intrigued. As the summer passes, Cole finds himself burning both ends of the candle to keep up with his job and his new relationship. **When he unleashes the Beast one time too many, Berlin will have to decide if she can tame him or if she should walk away.**

Get cowboy brothers working together at a horse farm in beautiful Vermont in the Steeple Ridge Farm romance series! With sweet, clean, and faith-filled western romance in a complete series, you'll get a cowboy billionaire, friends to lovers romance, holiday romance, and second chance romance with fun and unique plots (aquaponics, anyone?).

Her Billionaire Cowboy (Book 1): Tucker Jenkins has had enough of tall buildings, traffic, and has traded in his technology firm in New York City for Steeple Ridge Horse Farm in rural Vermont. Missy Marino has worked at the farm since she was a teen, and she's always dreamed of owning it. **Will Tucker and Missy be able to navigate the shaky ground between them to find a new beginning?**

About Liz

Liz Isaacson writes inspirational romance, usually set in Texas, or Wyoming, or anywhere else horses and cowboys exist. She lives in Utah, where she writes full-time, takes her two dogs to the park everyday, and eats a lot of veggies while writing. Find her on her website, along with all of her pen names, at feelgoodfictionbooks.com.